THE DIRT COURT

The Dirt Court

A novel
by

JOHNNY BELL

Adelaide Books
New York / Lisbon
2020

THE DIRT COURT
A novel
By Johnny Bell

Copyright © by Johnny Bell
Cover design © 2020 Adelaide Books

Published by Adelaide Books, New York / Lisbon
adelaidebooks.org

Editor-in-Chief
Stevan V. Nikolic

For any information, please address Adelaide Books
at info@adelaidebooks.org

or write to:

Adelaide Books
244 Fifth Ave. Suite D27
New York, NY, 10001

ISBN: 978-1-953510-81-5

Printed in the United States of America

Sarah, my wonderful wife.

Mom and Slop Pop.

To the students and players I've taught and

coached over the years

Acknowledgements

Sarah - thank you for encouraging and believing me! Your on-going love and support is special. I'm so blessed to have you in my life. Thank you for loving, supporting, and believing in me with every venture or challenge that comes our way.

Henry & Jennifer Banker - thank you for the love and support! Miss your great jokes, Jennifer!

Bonnie & Gloria, my work mother and auntie - you've always guided me and helped keep me focused. I couldn't ask for better Christian examples in a challenging workplace.

The students and players - I hope the stories I tell represent the challenges that you all have faced. I hope to bring honor, respect, and love to you all. I pray that each of you are off to wonderful tasks and accept the challenge to become great!

Chapter 1

Travis Mitchell was tired. Not from the forty-five minute bus ride to school, the irritating teachers throughout the school day, or even the aggravation of meeting new kids at school and trying to see where he fit in. After two weeks, he felt at ease in Easton, Alabama.

The tortuous night years ago constantly replayed in his head.

Bump, bump... bump, bump.

The best part of the day was the morning commute. The hum of the bus over country roads, students half-asleep and the sun playing a playful game of peak-a-boo through the trees felt so peaceful, so inviting.

"It's nice, huh?" Jarel flopped into the seat across the aisle from Travis. He took a deep breath and rested his back against the window.

"What's up, dude," replied Travis. He reached over and slapped hands with Jarel. "I'm still getting used to the scenery." He lived in lots of places across the Dixie State plenty of times but never a place like Garden County.

One thing that Travis had in common with the kids at Raymond Blake Middle School was a love for sports, specifically basketball. Didn't matter to the other sixth graders that he was the only white kid that can play. He could get to the rim and lock down anyone.

"We're gonna see who is playing when we get to school," Jarel said. He stretched his arms.

"Sounds good." Travis slumped into his seat. His Golden State Warriors hoodie flowed down to dark blue jeans with a small rip above the knees. The high-water jeans matched the worn-out, low-cut blue and yellow Steph Curry Adidas athletic shoes he had on. The tips on the laces were faded and there were scuff marks along the sides.

Travis looked at the rip in his jeans and thought back to the violent nights at the group home with Ms. Bermas. He tried to keep from getting angry. But he was always on verge of blowing up with rage.

"I expect you to hit your shots like you did last week." Jarel pointed his head down. A silly frown grew over his face.

"I got you man," Travis shook his head, chuckling.

"Just because you're new doesn't mean those kids are gonna cut you a break. It's still basketball. Eighty-four feet by fifty feet! Well, smaller court here, but still big in our hearts!" Jarel Pressell turned out to be just as smart off the court as he was on the court. "Did you work on your handles? You can't just be another white boy with a pretty shot. You gotta handle the rock!"

"Jarel, did you forget about how I crossed up that dude my first day there?"

"Of course not. But everyone here knows that Lamar is the *worst* defender at school. He's like the James Harden of Garden County *and* he can't shoot. He's so bad, he played wide receiver during football season… and he can't even catch!"

The boys laughed, then leaned back in their seats as Travis turned to look out the window.

Travis was glad to be back in the quiet peacefulness of his world. But he couldn't focus on enjoying the sunrise anymore. He began reminiscing. Specifically, about that tragic night and the days, weeks, months, and now, years of misery that followed.

Another sucky day. Travis lifted his backpack as Bus 2382 arrived at school. *I haven't had a good day at school, ever. Why should today be any different?*

Nothing could pull him from this funk. Not ankle-breaking moves before school, hearing a funny joke from Dean Matts, or the three periods of school he shared with Jarel.

"Ready to hoop," Jarel said. It was more of a statement than a question.

"Yup." Travis looked focused.

"It's time for the Celtic show, Irving and Hayward on stage." Jarel was hyped. The boys walked towards the outdoor basketball courts next to an old, brick gym.

"Competition has arrived." Lamar's cupped hands around his mouth helped the volume magnify. Warm air visible as he yelled.

"Are y'all ready to lose again?" Jarel took his backpack and jacket off and scooped up a ball and dribbled around. "I got my boy Travis. Who else is running with us?"

Travis rolled up the sleeves of his hoodie. His bright, blue Warriors hoodie wouldn't go on the ground like other kids did with their coats. This was too new and precious. A late Christmas gift from Alan and Virginia, the last family he stayed with before they grew tired of his behavior.

Maybe their comfortable, suburban life was too much for Travis. It reminded him of his dreams. Like playing organized sports, something that he'd never done. His whole life was a nightmare to others but a harsh reality to himself.

He looked around. He already learned some names in a couple weeks. Jarel, Lamar, Chris, James, and Jaden.

No need to memorize more, he thought. *I won't be here much longer.*

Jarel checked the ball with a dark-skin, tall black kid wearing a long-sleeve plaid button-down shirt and cargo pants. He took two dribbles before he decided his move. He started to drive to the goal with his left hand but quickly spun around to his right. As he took a dribble in the lane, a kid neglected his job of guarding Travis and ran over to stop Jarel.

Big mistake; he doesn't know who I am, Travis thought. He sprinted from the corner down the baseline toward the rim. Jarel made a beautiful bounce pass catching Travis in stride.

As he began the lay-up, Jarel's defender tried to jump to block the shot. Travis double-clutched the ball and scooped it off the opposite side of the rim with his left hand for a pretty reverse lay-up.

"Look at my boy getting buckets! One-nothing!" The duo exchanged high-fives.

The next possession was more of the same for Alabama's middle school version of the Celtics: Jarel dribbled to the left side of the court as Travis set a screen. Both defenders went to trap Jarel. He stepped between them and made a one-hand bounce pass to Travis.

Travis caught, took a dribble and slapped the backboard with both hands as the ball kissed the backboard for another point.

"Come on, now. This is too easy!" Jarel smiled as large as a classic Magic Johnson photo. "We gotta get this kid playing in the rec league with us next year. Chris, I got you next play. Y'all get ready on defense!"

A twenty-foot jumper by Chris cut through the cool morning air ripping the net.

Swish!

"Ones and twos, right? We're up four-zip." Jarel pointed to Chris as he pointed back. "Next basket is a skunk. Game over." Another drive to the rim ended with the athletic, chatty point guard scoring the fifth straight point.

"Game!" Jarel walked around and stuck out his chest with a grin on his face. "Y'all ready to run it back?" Steam rushed from Jarel's mouth as he spoke.

"New five, kid," George Franks walked up. He was the toughest basketball opponent Travis had ever faced. A giant as a 6'5" eighth grader and star of the Tigers' middle school boys' basketball and football team. Big, broad shoulders and a deep voice loomed.

"I thought seventh graders weren't allowed on the courts," he added.

"This court is for anyone that can hoop. That skunk game means we earned our spot. We get ball first." Jarel checked the ball with one of George's teammates.

"Oh, okay." George's tone was dripping with sarcasm.

Jarel and Travis were the only two kids in Garden County that weren't intimidated by George's size or skills.

But George didn't compare with the Four K's that Travis feared while living with Ms. Bermas in Hoover. *That* was misery. His fists clenched as he tensed up.

"Let's ball!" Jarel's cheer was just enough to snap Travis out of the daze and refocus him on the challenge ahead.

Here we go. Big foe. Big game. My chance to prove I can play, Travis thought. In his mind, the stage was set. Real game. Referees. Jerseys. Fans. Parents. Concessions.

Travis snapped back to the moment in front of him. Perfect timing – Jarel rocketed a one-hand pass towards Travis' face. Who caught the ball, spun around and lofted a soft hook-shot with his right hand. It bounced around on the rim from side to side before stumbling through the net.

BONG! Bong! The cold air forced the backboard and rim to echo while the boys prepared for the next play.

After George tied the score 1-1, Jarel rolled his eyes. Travis stared back blankly. Although new best friends, he didn't know what Jarel was thinking.

I guess he just means it's time to turn up, thought Travis. *First time we've had to play defense... Wait, does he want me to guard George?!*

"You got George," Jarel stated.

Shoot. That dude is huge! Travis stared at this freak of nature that wore size 13 Lebrons.

"Uh, okay." Travis tried to decide where to stand.

Brrring! Brrring!

Glad the bell rang! he thought.

George looked back and smiled. "Saved by the bell, huh?" He grabbed his backpack and walked toward a small stairway. Then turned around and shouted, "There's always tomorrow."

"You know what this means? We gotta work on your defense. You gonna guard George next time we play. Like, tomorrow." Jarel patted Travis' shoulder as the boys walked to class.

Jeez, here we go. Underdog, again. His mind drifted back to a dark place and that horrific night.

"Let's go, fellas," Dean Matts shouted from the walkway above.

As Jarel and Travis walked closer, he continued. "I saw you boys dominate the first game. Get your skills up so you can run with George. If you can hang with him, you have a chance to make the team next year, maybe even play high school ball in a couple years."

Middle school team? Next year? High school basketball? Be serious. I never even played organized ball! And you're talking about playing in high school? Travis thought.

"Even you, Mitchell. It doesn't matter if you never played organized ball before. There's something special in you. You just gotta decide if you're going to shine in the light or grow in the darkness."

What is he talking about? Shining in the light or growing in the darkness? This really is the Bible belt.

"Don't overthink it, man," Jarel said. "Dean Matts is good people. He's aight."

"Oh. Thanks man. Yeah, he seems cool." Travis looked up at Jarel before quickly looking back forward towards the floor.

His mind wandered between Dean Matts's comments, his new foster home with the Moorings, and that fateful night.

While the Moorings seemed caring, Travis wasn't ready to get too comfortable.

Everyone seems nice in the beginning. The families, schools, and kids. It's a "new person" phase or something. Just give it some time, he thought. *It won't be long until Diane and Craig get tired of calls from school and me living with them.*

Travis had the system all figured out. But this place was different. It wasn't like anywhere he'd been before. He didn't know if he meant that in a good way or not.

Chapter 2

Ms. Diane Mooring stood on the porch waiting. Travis and Jon hopped off the bus. Unknown to the boys, she already had a list of their homework assignments and chores written for their afternoon.

"Dude, is she going to be there every afternoon?" Travis asked Jon as they walked up the gravel road to the house. Her warm demeanor masked the drill sergeant she mimicked at home.

"Yup. Don't even think about trying anything slick. They're tougher and smarter than you think. They've been doing this for years," Jon advised. "But they are both good people. They'll look out for you. Just don't do anything stupid."

The boys continued walking closer to the porch, within earshot range of Ms. Diane.

Jon whispered, "And don't ever try Mr. Craig. He's worse than her."

"Hey fellas! How was your day?" Ms. Diane waved and smiled, showing her pearly white teeth. Her brown eyes sparkled on the cloudy afternoon. A dark blue denim jacket hung over the shoulders of her petite frame, covered with a mix of straight, brown and grey hair.

"Hey Ms. Diane," Jon replied. He seemed disinterested in their conversation, but obliged.

Travis watched, amused at how this small lady had her way with extracting information. His mind shifted to his own questions more than eavesdropping into their conversation, or interrogation, it seemed.

He didn't get it. *Why would this big, burly seventeen year-old junior allow a little old lady to force him to talk? Soon he'd be eighteen. Free to do and go wherever he wanted.* But Jon seemed content. Living here on State Road 43, outside the small town of Easton, Alabama with a handful of traffic lights.

Travis was quickly realizing that Jon was nothing like the other guys he lived with, especially Kage and Kedrick. But he kept his guard up, just in case there was an afternoon when the two boys were left home alone and Jon showed an evil side of himself.

Before Travis could sneak by, Ms. Diane shifted her focus to him. She smiled.

"I heard that you have something to share about your day?"

"Me? Nah. Nothing really, just another boring day."

"No... *ma'am*." Her stare intensified.

Travis stood his ground. He wouldn't give in like Jon. He was ready to go in the house, but felt as if he hadn't said the right password. He looked down, then around but still felt her eyes peering. *Dude... how long is this gonna last?* he thought.

"Ah, it's water under a bridge, honey. Come on!" She waived her hand. While he walked by, she placed a hand on his shoulder. Travis jumped back as if he was dodging a right hook.

Ms. Diane let out a chuckle. "Hah! Don't get your britches all bunched up, now!"

"I'm gonna start on my homework." Travis quickly walked through the front doorway. He barely opened his math book before Jon popped into his room. Nicely-made bedsheets bunched as he slid onto the bed and sprawled out.

"You know you messed up. Don't worry, she isn't gonna starve you or take your stuff. But I am warning you, if you mess this up for me then you'll have another problem."

"I'm so scared!" Travis pretended to bite his fingernails.

Ms. Diane knocked and leaned in. "Hey boys. Travis, come here for a minute, please."

He looked over at Jon then Ms. Diane. He thought about saying that he had a lot of homework, that he was really tired.

"Excuse me," Jon quickly hurried off to his room.

"This way," she said as she walked away. Travis followed her to the kitchen island. She had a bag of dark greens and a large pot of boiling water sitting on the stove.

"Go and wash your hands over there. Then start ripping the stems off and place them in the pot." Ms. Diane turned her back to Travis as she began pulling random ingredients down from the cupboard.

"What's this, cabbage?" Travis began ripping this soft, spongy-like lettuce into tiny pieces.

She laughed, "No, baby. You never had collard greens?!"

"No." He corrected himself and added *ma'am* the second time.

She turned back to check his progress. "Oh, not like that, honey. Just the stems. Mr. Craig loves collard greens! I reckon I learned to like them too after being married all this time."

Travis had no idea why she made him help. He never did this in the other places he lived. Still pondering, he continued pulling apart the greens, this time, by the stem.

"You mind if I put some music on? I love some good tunes."

"Nah... I mean, no ma'am. It's your house." Travis didn't look up.

"Well, technically it's Mr. Craig *and* my house. Since you and Jon are here, it's your home too." She patted Travis on the back as she walked over to turn on a wireless speaker.

What? That's Tupac! Travis' head popped up as the track played. He was shocked that an old white lady listened to rap music. She turned the volume up a little louder from her phone.

"Ms. Diane," his voice cracked. "What do you know about Tupac?"

"Oh honey, I don't know much about him. Just do like Tupac says, listen to the words!" She continued pouring flour and milk and mixing in her bowl. The music echoed down the halls.

Travis spent the next hour following orders – mixing ingredients, pouring spices, and mostly stirring the greens. The kitchen smelled wonderful. The scent of cornbread and baked chicken forced Travis into a lull, as if Ms. Diane had cast a spell over him.

The next evening, Mr. Craig showed Travis around their property. His bald head shined with the sunset. His red button-down shirt untucked from stylish jeans matched the red and gold Kyrie Irving *Flytrap* basketball shoes. The kicks seemed oversized and odd for a short black guy that had a bit of a country slang when he spoke.

A basketball goal hung on the side of the barn. The rectangle above the rim was faded. But a new, chain net was inviting.

"You play?" Mr. Craig continued walking towards the barn, his back to Travis.

"Oh, yeah… Yes sir." He turned to catch up. *Who would shoot out here? Decent goal but who'd play on a dirt court? This isn't Hoosiers.*

"Maybe I'll show you how to hoop," he hollered. "Help me open this door, please."

The two pushed a wide aluminum door that rolled up like a garage door. Inside the rustic building were some four-wheelers, a backhoe, and a utility trailer. There were lots of tools for doing yardwork when the weather warmed up, Mr. Craig informed.

The ATVs were the same colors with opposite painting schemes; one was mostly dark green with yellow highlights. *Smash* was written in black letters and outlined in white. The other was yellow with dark green accents and trim pieces. The yellow four-wheeler had *Hoops* written in white letters with black outlines.

Matching four-wheelers. For the odd couple.

Mr. Craig cranked up both four-wheelers and pointed to the yellow ATV while he hopped on *Smash*. No words, no instructions.

Go figure. I get the yellow one, and I don't even know how to drive. At least it has a basketball nickname on it, he tried to be positive.

It didn't take long for Travis to catch on. They rode around for about an hour, exploring twenty beautiful, untamed acres of woods, hills and streams.

If only everyday could be as relaxing as this.

"*Ring!*" Travis jumped from his seat. He was about to doze off in fifth period math class.

"Mrs. Ranson, we need Travis Mitchell in the front office," said the secretary.

"He's on the way." She turned to Travis. "Take that sheet home and finish it. Have Ms. Diane call me if you need any help."

"Yes, ma'am." Hurriedly, he gathered his work before hustling down the hall. *Are they moving me already? Did Diane and Craig get tired of me?*

Over the past four years, Travis bounced around to different group homes. He marked the time by Valentine's Day. It was that night that everything came crashing down. His world went dark. His mind drifted back to that evening.

Fears turned to frustration as he entered the office.

Travis saw Lincoln Arnold sitting next to the secretary. *Ugh, him again.* He already knew the drill. This was just another welfare check, a mundane task whenever a kid was placed in a new home.

Lincoln rose from his seat and reached to shake hands with the irritated sixth grader. "Hey Travis."

"Hey." Travis hardly made eye contact.

His case manager was kinda cool. He loved basketball, was funny, and liked playing video games. Both guys were in the foster care system in Alabama. Like Travis, he had a couple bumps along the road. Two arrests landed him in juvenile court. The second time in handcuffs and an ultimatum from the judge was enough to scare Lincoln straight, he shared with Travis.

The two moved to an adjacent conference room. Lincoln cleared his throat as they sat in office chairs. "So, no bad news or anything. Here to check on you and see how things are going."

"It's okay," Travis answered.

"Okay? Like *okay, I'm ready to talk*? Or like *okay, it's all good*?" Lincoln crossed his legs.

"Come on, Lincoln. I thought you were cool." One smiled. But the other sighed. "It's okay. They feed me. I have my own bed. I have my own room. Oh, I also have my own chores!"

Disappointment covered Lincoln's face.

Travis rolled his eyes while his mentor sat quietly, waiting. "I'm not doing any chores. That's for sure. I don't care what you say."

Lincoln leaned back in his chair. His eyes focused. The youngster couldn't handle the stare and looked off. He slouched in his chair.

"Well? Isn't this where you tell me that I '*need to do what they ask so I don't get moved again*' or '*I won't get many more chances.*'"

"Nah man, I'm not doing that. You know the drill. You know what's next."

"Okay then! So why are we here? Why are we doing this?" He didn't have anyone in his life that cared. Due to Lincoln's workload, they only met once a month. Over the past four years Lincoln was the closest thing Travis had.

"You know what the alternative is, but I don't think you realize how good it could go with Ms. Diane and Mr. Craig," Lincoln said. "Hey, have you asked Jon what the Moorings are like?"

"Yes. Jon is whipped. He says and does whatever they want."

"Not quite. He's seventeen, right? Do you know what happens when he turns eighteen?"

"Yeah, he can go and do whatever he wants."

"Eh, *kinda*… Once eighteen, he's considered an adult. That means Mr. Craig and Ms. Diane legally don't have to keep him in their home. What will he do if they tell him to move?"

"Get a job."

"Yeah, he can. How will he get money for rent, groceries, car insurance?"

"From working. Duh."

"Have you talked with Jon about what he's going to do next year?"

"No. He has one more year of… high school." It slowly dawned on Travis. *Jon turns eighteen this summer. He could skip his last year of high school and start working. But if he wants to finish high school?* He tried to sound calm, "He'll probably get a football scholarship or something."

"You're right. Hopefully he can. You should talk to him."

They sat in silence for what seemed like an eternity.

"So, have you seen their goal?" Lincoln changed the topic.

"Basketball hoop?"

"Yeah, the one at the house!"

"Oh, that old raggedy thing with a dirt court?" Travis rolled his eyes.

"Yes, man! That court is for ballers. Only the best play there!"

"What do you mean? You played on that busted up goal before?"

"Well, yeah! Wait, you haven't even *shot* out there yet? And you claim to be a baller." Lincoln shook his head, smiling.

Travis crossed his arms and swiveled side to side on the chair.

"You gotta get out there, man. Did you know that Ms. Diane can hoop? Mr. Craig can too, but Ms. Diane, whew. She can shoot!"

Travis realized there were lots of things he didn't know. *Maybe there's some neat stuff in this little town. Maybe Jarel would be a good friend. He'd been helpful and cool so far. After the ATVs and cooking experience, maybe Mr. Craig and Ms. Diane would be okay.*

While Travis' list of questions outweighed answers, one thing that seemed sure – Ms. Diane and Mr. Craig had Travis' back.

But that devotion and support would soon be tested.

Chapter 3

Travis snuck outside to inspect the basketball goal at the Mooring's home. After finishing chores and homework. He tussled around inside the barn to see if he could find a ball.

"Looking for this?" Ms. Diane asked.

Travis's heart skipped a beat. He slowly stood from a crouching position behind a rolling tool cart. "Oh, uh, I didn't know you were here." *I bet she thinks I'm trying to steal something.*

She tossed a gift wrapped in blue paper, in the shape of a sphere.

"Here, open it up!" she said. A huge smile grew on her face.

He steadily tossed the present from hand to hand, unsure if he should tear off the wrapping paper. Unwrapping the gift unlocked a pastime to the only place he felt safe.

He hesitated, and finally looked up. Then began pacing around. *Where'd she go?*

Chingling! Something outside rattled.

He walked out the barn, following the sound.

Boing, boing! Chingling!

"Ah, I've always preferred the sound of chains over the pop of the net. I guess it's the city in me!" Ms. Diane chased a worn-out Spalding basketball. It bounced toward the side of the barn. As she picked up her ball, she turned around. Travis stared.

"Don't expect a pass from me. I was born to shoot. I never cared much about assists." She took another shot from about twenty feet away, near the top of the key.

She released the ball at the highest point of her jump, with perfect form and the dirty-orange Spalding rotated perfectly through the air. No rim, all net.

Chingling!

"Such a beautiful sound!" Smiling, she jogged to pick up the ball. "If you're just going to stand there, you might as well rebound for me!"

Another jumper splashed the chains. This one bounced off the front of the rim, kissed the backboard and dropped through.

Travis hustled to keep giving her the ball. He'd been taken back to his younger days of rebounding for his uncle at the park. He remembered how mesmerized he'd been by Uncle Eddy's ability to shoot.

His mind bounced between the past and the present. Happy moments at the park when Uncle Eddy would play one-on-one. Travis had ran around in an old, oversized dark blue Stephen Curry jersey. A white Golden Gate Bridge with gold trim. It was his only basketball jersey.

He could picture Uncle Eddy chasing him around the black hardtop on a bright sunny day. Travis would take a couple dribbles while his uncle gave him a light tug. He'd swipe at the ball, giving enough effort for the eight year-old to believe he was really trying to play. He missed those days.

"Whew! That feels good!" She pounded the worn-down ball on the cool dirt. "Here, take some shots. I heard you can play." She drilled a chest pass with more strength than he expected.

"Umph!" He winced, then bobbled the ball.

"Haha, old Sojo is harsh on you fellas!" She walked towards the basket and chuckled. "Are you gonna shoot or stand there looking pretty?"

Travis rushed a shot. His first three shots were way off. The first bounced hard off the front of the rim, nearly taking out Ms. Diane. The second one slammed from the backboard then ricocheted off the basket, and bouncing back to him. He sighed before launching a third brick. This one nearly wedged itself between the rim and backboard.

"Dude, you're making Dean Matts and Jarel look bad. They said you could play. Take a couple dribbles, get a feel for the court." She made a bounce pass. "Maybe it's the intimidation of this court. Craig warned me!"

He took a couple dribbles. The first bounce was too soft. Then the second bounce was too hard. The ball nearly hit him in the face.

"You know, this old dirt court is kind of like life, for some people," she added.

He continued to dribble. While trying to get a feel for the lifeless ball, he waited for Ms. Diane to finish her thought.

"Shoot!" She waved her hands in the air.

This time Travis focused on his form. This shot from fifteen feet out on the left side. The chain shook. Another basket, another pass. In one smooth motion, he caught the ball, took a dribble with his left hand and delivered another chain-rattling jumper. She executed perfect passes, from one shooter to another. He could tell because she tossed the ball in rhythm, to the shooter's pocket.

After a few minutes, he broke the harmony of rattling the chains and pounding the ball on the dirt. "Who is *Sojo*?"

"That's what you're shooting with." She laughed. "That's who I named the ball after!"

"Why *Sojo*?" He made a beautiful behind-the-back move and launched another shot.

"Oh Lord. You've never heard of Sojourner Truth?!" She stopped.

He felt small, as if the answer was that obvious. It was like not knowing that Kareem Abdul-Jabbar is the leading scorer in NBA history, or Bill Russell has the most championships rings.

"No, never heard of her." Travis clanked a shot off the side of the rim.

"We'll work on it. So much to learn." Her voice level went up and down as she chased the ball. "I'm not used to rebounding so many missed shots!"

After another long school day, Travis was happy to flop into his bus seat. He pulled his hood over his unkempt hair, hoping to take a nap during the thirty-minute ride home.

"What up, Squeaks?" Brooke walked down the bus aisle and sat behind him. She looked over at Jarel across the aisle and nodded her head. Her curly, brown hair bounced against her cinnamon cheeks. Today's outfit was the same faded denim jacket she had worn every day.

Kelsey nudged her towards the window so she could sit down. Bolder than her cousin, the right side of her head was shaved, with a star design. But equally as talented on the softball field. She wore a long sleeve, black and gold Saints shirt.

"Yo. Sup, B," Jarel said. "When are y'all gonna hop on the court and go two-on-two with me and my boy, Travis?" Jarel looked at Kelsey and smiled.

"Just because you've got game on the court, doesn't mean you got enough to talk to me." Kelsey rolled her eyes.

"Ouch! Squeaks, how much more can you take?" Brooke laughed.

Jarel batted his eyes and fanned himself like he was about to faint. "As much love as she can share!"

"Why do you call him *Squeaks*?" Travis tried to come to Jarel's defense.

"Well, Q, that's a really good *question*. Here, the answer will lie in the question I ask you. Don't you pay attention to how he talks?" Brooke raised her eyebrows and gave a pointed look.

Travis looked at her and contemplated. *Why does she call me* Q?

"Let me guess, you have another question!" Brooke said.

Kelsey chuckled as Travis started to turn around to ignore both girls.

"For real, B. You're that one ugly friend blocking the guy from talking to the cute friend." Jarel laughed. "The only difference is that y'all are cousins, I'm not sure how."

"If I had a dollar for every time you said something dumb..." Brooke began.

"It wouldn't be as much money if I had a *dime* for every time *you* said something stupid." Jarel nearly fell out his seat laughing. He almost received a boot to the head from Kelsey if the bus driver hadn't glanced up in the mirror to catch the group's attention.

Jarel and Kelsey sat up in their seats across the aisle from each other.

"Thank you!" Mrs. Rachel shouted back towards them. The two gave the bus driver artificial grins.

"Brooke, let's make a bet," Jarel continued. "If I beat you in a game of *Elephant*, you sit on the bus quietly for a week."

"Elephant?" Brooke looked at Kelsey. Both girls shrugged their shoulders.

"Yes. *Elephant* instead of *Horse*, because you talk too much. That's a hard word for you to spell. But easy for you to imagine. Just look in the mirror!" He laughed hard but didn't fall from his seat.

"Or we could play a game called *Dodge THIS!*" Brooke said.

"Dodge *what?*"

"Dodge *this!*" She threw pens and pencils across the aisle. Between throws she yelled, "Ready… to… call… mercy?"

"Okay!" He hollered while trying to block.

Travis shook his head. *These kids were nearly as dysfunctional as the group home where I lived in 5th grade. The only difference is that these kids aren't as evil as the boys I had to live with.* He lost count of how many times Swirlies or Wet Willies he received that year.

He could recall the weekly routine after Ms. Bermas ordered *lights out.* The boys tied Travis in his bedsheet and played a game of 'pillow tag.' They'd take shots at each other with their pillows. Then peg him with body blows to signal a change in rounds.

Just *thinking* of Ms. Bermas filled him with rage. Vengeance filled his soul with bitterness. Not only did the misery and pain flood in, but sadness as well. He thought of a plan to get even with Brooke, to take out the frustration on her that he hadn't given to the older boys and their pillows. Instead, she would serve as his punching bag.

Instinctively, he put down his window and grabbed Brooke's backpack from her lap. As she tried to struggle for it, he outmuscled her and threw it out the window. *That'll teach her to mess with people.*

"Hey!" Brooke screamed. Jarel turned to see the backpack fly outside.

Travis looked back at Brooke. Her eyes welled up and her jaw shuddered. Tears slowly dropped. He looked to the back of the bus to see Jon shaking his head in irritation. He messed up but couldn't apologize now, it was too late. He had to be tough, at least look it.

Before sitting down, he felt a sharp sting on his left cheek. Kelsey delivered a strong blow. She followed with a stinking, open-hand slap. Before Travis could regain his stance, Jarel hopped across the aisle and bear-hugged Travis as he pulled him back to his seat.

Erupting with rage, he tried to shake himself free. Before he could fight back, Jon stood over him. His fire dimmed as the scene became clear. Mrs. Rachel stirred the bus off the highway.

"Don't move!" Jon pointed.

"Don't tell me what to do! I ain't scared of you!" Travis yelled back as he continued to squirm within Jarel's grasp.

"You're being stupid!" His older foster brother walked to the front of the bus.

Travis heard some high school students in the back grumble about the delay. Heard Jon plead with Mrs. Rachel not to go back to school. They're almost home. But he really didn't care, about anything or anyone. Then he looked at Brooke for the first time since the melee began.

She cried as Kelsey wrapped an arm around her shoulder. Brooke really wasn't a mean-hearted or evil person. She'd been as nice as a twelve year-old girl could be the new kid on the block. Maybe it was her natural instinct to protect her cousin, Kelsey.

Within minutes a red Charger wrapped in yellow stripes with "Garden County" written on the side pulled up behind the bus with lights flashing.

"Woooo!" the kids laughed. "It's Deputy Crews! That boy's in trouble! That's the wrong cop to mess with! That's Mrs. Rachel's beau!" One kid yelled, "They gonna make out real quick!"

Mrs. Rachel blushed as she tried to hush the students.

But Travis wasn't smiling. He wasn't angry anymore either. He'd been in trouble before. But never with the law.

Chapter 4

Mrs. Rachel continued to discuss the incident with Deputy Crews. A black and silver sheriff truck pulled up in front of the parked bus. Lights flickered. More *Oooh's* swept through the bus.

"Just take him so we can go home!" shouted a high schooler.

Travis and Jarel remained in their seat. Jon sat in the front row behind Mrs. Rachel's seat. While the adults talked, Deputy Crews stared intensely at Travis. A tight, gray *GCSO* polo exposed his huge biceps. The badge was worn on the left side of his belt. A firearm hung on the right.

Kelsey appeared to be just as terrified as Travis. He remembered that she hit him in the face, but feared that he'd be in more trouble for starting the brawl.

Travis checked his watch. They'd been parked for twenty minutes. Two cars were pulling up, one of them he recognized. Ms. Diane hopped out of her dark blue Expedition. As she walked towards the bus, a black Toyota Tundra with big tires parked behind her. A short white guy wearing a red *Garden County Baseball* polo and black sunglasses. He got out and jogged to the bus.

"Oh snap! That's Dean Matts's truck!" another high school student hollered from the back. She looked at Travis with an evil smirk.

His heart dropped. Lincoln warned him about not messing up at the Moorings. *Why didn't I listen?*

While the adults discussed the incident, the students' grumbling escalated to horseplay. But it ceased as Dean Matts climbed onto the bus. He greeted some of the students, then walked towards the middle of the bus. "Hey guys, call your parents, let them know the bus is running late." He looked at Travis. "Come with me. Kelsey, we'll talk tomorrow." Then turned back to Brooke. "Was there anything valuable in there? Cell phone, a tablet?"

"No- no sir," she whimpered. Her head down. "I don't have a phone."

"Okay. I'm gonna let the bus get going. We'll walk down the road to find your backpack."

Travis dropped his head and slowly walked down the aisle to meet his fate. He kept his tough demeanor amid the laughs and jeers from his peers. There was a mix of cheers and laughs from students as Mrs. Rachel fired up the engine.

"See you round, Diane." The deputy said, climbing into his black and silver police truck.

"Bye, honey!" She didn't seem the least bothered by the incident.

Unfortunately Deputy Crews and Dean Matts didn't share the same feelings as Ms. Diane. She asked Jon if he wanted to help look for the backpack or wait in the truck. But Jon flopped in the front seat and glared at Travis.

"Well, hurry up, honey! It's cold out here and you got chores to help with!" She turned and walked towards the Expedition.

Travis glanced at the two men. Deputy Crews seemed as big as NBA star Zion Williamson with his flat-top hairdo. Dean Matts's short, blonde hair and build made him look like a muscular version of Lincoln.

"You need to hustle. I have to get back for a high school game soon," Dean Matts ordered.

Travis adjusted his backpack and began walking through the overgrown grass near the ditch past Ms. Diane's truck. She smiled and waved.

Travis' shifted to worrying about riding in the back seat of Deputy Crews' patrol car. He'd heard horror stories from older kids in foster care about riding with cops.

After walking up and down the road for about fifteen minutes, Dean Matts pointed to a pink bag in the ditch. "That's it. How far do you think we've walked?"

"Close to a mile," Deputy Crews replied.

"Shoot, I'm going to be late over this." He looked back at Travis. "Hurry up and grab the bag!"

Travis picked up Brooke's backpack. There were grass stains and mud all over it and a hole on the side. He remembered how nice it looked before. It was a fancy pink *PB Teen* backpack with two female basketball players on the side that wrapped around to the front. Some of her belongings fell out as Travis tried to pick it up. The two adults shook their heads.

"Just get the stuff in there somehow." Dean Matts flailed his hands in the air.

Travis remembered hearing the girls talking about Brooke's backpack last week. It was a Christmas gift. He knew how precious it was to her.

"Hand it to Deputy Crews," Dean Matts stated as the guys approached three parked vehicles along the ghostly road. "I'll see you in my office first thing tomorrow morning." He walked to the Expedition and spoke with Ms. Diane in low tones before taking off.

She seemed oblivious to the incident as the three of them rode the last stretch of State Road 43. She spoke casually about dinner plans that evening and the possible weekend trip to visit her sister in Pensacola.

"The beach may be a little too cold, though! What do you think, Travis?" She peeked in the mirror as she parked. "We'll figure it out. We're also gonna talk about what happened." They climbed out of the truck. "Get your homework done and rest up. It's been quite a day."

As they were finishing dinner, Jon excused himself and Ms. Diane began packing lunches. *No one said anything about what happened on the bus today. I can't believe it. Maybe, I-*

"Have you thought about how you're gonna make up with Brooke?" Mr. Craig asked.

"No." Travis stared straight ahead. In his mind he'd already found a way. *Just tip-toe back to the room and pretend to be asleep.*

"*Sir,*" added Ms. Diane. She looked away from the counter to correct him.

"No, sir." He hesitated.

Mr. Craig rubbed his scruffy beard. "Get started on a list. We'll talk in a little bit." He stood up and began helping Ms. Diane in the kitchen.

A list of what? Things that I'm going to do for Brooke? List of more chores that I'm going to do for you guys?! She's the one that was messing with Jarel! That called me 'Q'! He stopped midway down the hall, grabbed his jacket and snuck out the backdoor.

He wasn't going to work on any stupid *list*. It wasn't even his fault! The girls were the ones that started the whole thing. Kelsey calling people names, then Brooke throwing pencils at Jarel. He was simply helping Jarel as the girls ganged up on him. And no one had said anything about Kelsey throwing punches at Travis!

He headed towards the one thing that gave him relief. Basketball.

Yes! Lights! He hopped down the back steps and looked around to see if he could find the ball Ms. Diane gave him. It wasn't against the wall. Not next to the barn. Nor in the back porch. Not anywhere. *All I want to do is shoot and I can't find a stupid ball!* He kicked a small branch.

"It sucks when you can't find what you're looking for, huh?" a deep voice stated.

Travis jumped. Mr. Craig, still in his work clothes had a basketball in his hands, the same worn-out Spalding ball Ms. Diane was shooting earlier.

"I guess it's better than roaming around without a purpose," he continued. Then he walked towards the goal.

Travis followed him to the dirt court. *Let me guess, everyone in this family can play.*

"Shoot." Mr. Craig drilled a pass to Travis. He caught it with his chest. This time without wincing, like he'd done with Ms. Diane.

"Definitely not a wide receiver, huh?" Mr. Craig turned his back.

Anyone can drill a pass when someone isn't looking. He bounced the ball on the ground, then spun the ball on his hands and began to shoot.

Swish! Travis shot quietly while Mr. Craig kept feeding him the ball. It didn't take long to heat up. He was in the zone, hopping from spot to spot. The only sound was the ringing of chains and the pop of the worn-out ball as the crisp passes hit Travis' hands.

With every made basket, Travis' mind slipped further away from the dirt court, back to the hardtops at Smiley Court Apartments. That's where the only happy memories for Travis were- afternoons with Uncle Eddy shooting hoops.

Catch, rise, shoot, repeat. That's what Uncle Eddy said when Travis would ask him how he was such a good shooter. *Catch, rise, shoot, repeat,* Travis whispered and found himself doing it automatically. *Catch, rise, shoot, repeat. Catch, rise, shoot, repeat.*

"Good shooting, man! Keep it up!"

"Thanks, Uncle." Smiling, he took another shot.

"Huh?"

"What?" Travis took another shot. This one was off, breaking a streak of eleven jumpers in a row. It took him a second to realize he wasn't at the outdoor courts, not at his apartment complex of Smiley Court Community Center.

Now he was shooting on a dimly-lit dirt court, with two little overhead building lights. He began thinking Brooke, Kelsey and Jarel. About why he would do something that stupid. It wasn't like he didn't know right from wrong.

All his shots were off.

"Maybe you really *are* a football kid!" Mr. Craig chased a long rebound.

He caught the ball and heaved a rainbow shot. The ball bounced hard off the side of the rim, going to the opposite side of the goal from the previous attempt.

"Are we going to talk about it or what?" Frustration boiled. Mr. Craig was ruining the one thing he loved.

Mr. Craig chased down the ball and headed toward the house. Once at the steps, he turned around. "You gonna come in?"

Travis hesitated. But when Mr. Craig walked by and didn't even look at him, it made Travis crave *some* attention. He gave the same look as Uncle Eddy. *Come on, let's go man.*

The two sat on the porch. March evenings come quick and cold in central Alabama. Just as Travis was about to get up, the back door swung open.

Ms. Diane had two water bottles in her hand. "Here y'all go." She tossed each a bottle.

"Thank you, thanks," the guys replied, nearly in unison. She quickly disappeared into the warmth of the house.

"Look, I know I messed up," Travis began. "I don't know what I was thinking. I'm sorry." This is when he would say he understood, and Travis would be grounded or something.

"Mmm…" He sipped from his water bottle.

"Mmhmm and?" The sweaty, streaky shooter waited.

"You knew what you were doing. You're not ready to *talk* about what you were thinking."

Travis jumped back. *What did he really know about me? Did Mr. Craig know about Uncle Eddy? About that night?* He wanted to forget about everything. Not just that night – the *Boom!* The fire, smoke, Smiley Court Apartments. But about Ms. Bermas' and the K's, and that afternoon on the bus.

Ms. Diane and Mr. Craig knew what he wanted, and what he was about to do. Like they already knew more about him than *he* knew about himself.

"Do you remember what I said when you were looking for a ball in the barn?"

"No… sir."

"I said 'it's better than roaming around, without a purpose. You know, trying to figure out what you want'," he paraphrased.

Travis looked down at his water bottle. *What is this old fart talking about?* He took a sip of water. Mr. Craig was talking about having goals. *But what type of goals can you have when you're sent from house to house every couple of months?*

He wouldn't let anyone know, but Travis still dreamed, hoped, and prayed to be adopted. Not like he had much faith that it would happen. Kids his age that bounced around so much and that grew up on the wrong side of town weren't wanted by couples.

Mr. Craig finished his thought, "... so we're in this for the long-run, with you." He reached over to pat Travis on the shoulder like Uncle Eddy would do.

But Travis wasn't ready. He jumped back. His eyes bulged. There was an awkward pause between the two. Eyes locked onto each other with contrasting tales. Mr. Craig had a gentle look on his face while Travis looked uncomfortable, ashamed to have reacted that way. He began to apologize but was cut off.

"There's still going to be a consequence," Mr. Craig said, taking a sip of water.

As the back door swung open, Ms. Diane ushered Kelsey onto the porch. A crazy evening to follow a ridiculous afternoon.

Chapter 5

"Hey." Kelsey said, in a voice slightly above a whisper.

A slender lady nudged her onto the porch. "Well? That's a cold start." She looked over at the guys. "Hey there, Mr. Craig! How are ya?" She said, cheerfully.

"Hey, Bridgette." They embraced, paid no attention to the two middle schoolers. Adults have a way of ignoring kids when they're in trouble, then speak about the children like they weren't sitting right in front of them. He turned and hugged Kelsey. "I heard you had quite a bus ride. No Brooke?"

"She's with Ms. Diane." Bridgette replied, then turned toward Travis. "I'm Ms. Bridgette, Kelsey's mom and Brooke's auntie."

"Hey."

"Kelsey has something to say to you." She maintained an intense stare, hands resting on her hips, then pinched Kelsey's elbow.

"Ow! I was about to begin!" She rubbed her elbow gently and faced her new enemy.

Travis couldn't believe that Kelsey's mom dragged her over to the house. She hadn't had to hit Travis, although he may have deserved it. He was shocked that Brooke was even here. It wasn't her fault that Travis was stupid enough to throw her bag out the window.

"So… I'm sorry," Kelsey blurted out. She fidgeted, trying to squirm away from her mom. Her apology still not good enough.

"It's, it's no biggie. We're cool." Ms. Bridgette's firmness made his stomach feel queasy. Words fumbled around on his lips. "I, uh, shouldn't have started it."

"Let her finish!" Ms. Bridgette's head spun so quickly from Kelsey to Travis that he thought her neck might snap. She whispered commands with such authority that Travis' heart-beat soared higher than his player rating on *NBA 2K* on PlayStation 4.

The rattled girl altered her stance. She crossed her arms, shifting one leg straight and her body weight onto the other leg. Leaning away from her mother, she continued. "I shouldn't have punched you in the face, *twice*. Next time I will use my words to express how I feel," she concluded. The bit of sass in her comments with *twice* was quickly adjusted when she peaked over for her mother's approval.

Ms. Diane popped out onto the ghostly quiet porch before Ms. Bridgette could chime in. "Why don't y'all come inside? We can talk over a pot of coffee. Would you care for some?"

Ms. Bridgette turned from Kelsey and accepted the invitation into the warmth. Her face changed from a scowl to a smile.

"That's a good idea!" Ms. Bridgette beamed. "Maybe we could let the kids work it out."

"Good thinking, Bridgette." Ms. Diane waved for Kelsey's mother to join her, then turned around and motioned for Brooke to come outside. "Y'all hang out here. If you need anything just have Travis come in!" Travis slouched as the girls stood side-by-side.

As she let the door close, Kelsey gave an artificial grin to Ms. Diane. Then turned to Travis. "I did my part. Now, don't you have something to say to Brooke?" she snapped.

Great, here we go again. He slowly raised his head. An awkward game of avoiding eye contact ensued. *Man, I messed up.*

Brooke caught a glimpse of the basketball goal hanging from the side of the barn. The lights bounced off the old rim just enough to make a real *hooper* smile. *Hooper* was a made-up word Travis picked up in years ago while watching Uncle Eddy and older guys play at Smiley Community Center. *A hooper is anyone that can ball, loves to ball, and looks to play ball at any opportunity.* Travis tried explaining to the *Knucklehead Brothers, more like a gang of misfits.*

"You wanna shoot?" Travis wanted to do anything possible to make Brooke smile. Cancel out his stupid actions earlier that afternoon. He may not ever be able to persuade Brooke to like him, but he had to make up for what happened.

Brooke shrugged her shoulders. Kelsey grilled Travis, intently. He grabbed the worn-out basketball in one hand and took Brooke with his other hand. He smiled sheepishly as he pushed the screen door open with his back. She seemed reluctant, but allowed herself to be escorted.

Kelsey scoffed before settling into a cushioned, outdoor chair on the porch.

"So, do you want to shoot?" He tried to sound cheerful but not over the top, spinning the ball over his hands.

"Nah. I'm fine." Brooke crossed her arms and stood at the edge where the packed dirt blended with dead grass.

"Oh. Are you sure?" Travis' lowered his volume, slightly. He still hadn't apologized to her, nor addressed the biggest issue – her custom, torn-up backpack.

While holding the ball, he took a deep breath as spit rolled down the back of his throat. "Hey Brooke?" He asked, doing his best to sound sorry as possible, but not fake. Apologies weren't something that he heard often, especially genuine ones.

"Yeah?" Her head down. She didn't retreat as he stood less than a foot from her. Close enough for him to hug. But close enough for her to punch.

With the ball on his hip, he took another deep breath before suffering from word vomit. "I'm sorry... I don't know what I was thinking. That was really stupid of me, to throw your backpack. Sorry, I didn't mean to say it like that. I just... I was upset, and it really had nothing to do with you, or Kelsey. Well, I mean... I didn't like watching Jarel have pencils thrown at him... but he really shouldn't have been annoying you guys first. But still, it doesn't give me the right to throw your stuff out... I guess I need to stop bringing that up. I'm going to replace your backpack. It looked really nice, I mean, before the accident. Sorry, I..."

In mid-sentence Brooke turned around and headed to the house. He heard sniffling as she brought one hand to her face and the other swung as she hurried up the porch. Kelsey stood to greet her with open arms, then gave Travis a dirty look.

Bang! The screen door frame vibrated softly as the two girls sat down.

He didn't know what to do. He couldn't just turn around and start shooting, or sit with them on the porch. Brooke was too hurt and Kelsey was too volatile. And he definitely couldn't go back into the house, especially without the girls.

So he stood there. Feeling empty. Lonely. Like that night, flames had sizzled, with emergency workers all around. He stood with a blanket over his shoulders. Everything gone. No one to run to.

Can't remember the last time I was hugged. Oh yeah... on the day he'd met Ms. Diane. He recalled her asking if it was okay to give him a hug. He'd shook his head no. But deep inside, the answer was yes.

"That's okay. Whenever you're ready!" She'd gently shook his hand their first day together. He'd felt Lincoln's disappointment as the three of them left the agency center, down a bland, white hallway and out towards the main lobby with artificial plants. But there was no artificial love in her heart.

Over the time of Travis' stay, he'd fallen into her embrace. A pat on the back, leaning towards her short, welcoming frame for a side-hug, or allowing her soft hands to rub his head.

Man, two weeks seemed to have flown by.

His mind slipped back to Hoover, when he learned that this was going to be full of never-ending misery. It wasn't the third or fourth time the boys played 'pillow tag' at Travis' expense. Or the repeated noogies during the first week. By the end of the first month, Travis had been locked in a closet five times. He couldn't remember if it had been Kedrick or Korbin, or Kage who was usually the ringleader of the gang. As much as he hated them, it wasn't the darkness filling that filthy house that pained him the most. He remembered the loneliness.

Yet here he was, standing alone, in the dark. The lights from the barn hardly reached the edge of the dirt court, where weeds were creeping in. His silhouette covered the empty yard.

The backdoor burst open with laughter and banter as the adults tried to play down the joy from their fellowship inside. Unlike the torture that Kage, Kedrick, Kyron, and Korbin, the boys later opened the door to the closet, full of crude laughter.

Ms. Bridgette was the first one. Her smile shined long enough.

Like a volcano, the built-in fire was due to erupt. The humiliation of having to face Brooke and Kelsey, in front of his foster parents. Dealing with Ms. Bridgette's fierce, confrontational attitude.

He punted the ball as hard as he could. Curious, Ms. Diane came out of the house and asked what all the commotion was.

Fight.

Doesn't work. That's what got him in this situation to begin with. Losing control and lashing out at others was why he felt this way. Hurting others wouldn't help, especially Brooke. That creates bigger problems.

Flight. Run! Where? Anywhere but here.

He turned and sprinted towards the woods, beyond the barn. Running toward the darkness, away from the light and warmth he finally began to feel with the Moorings. But he messed up. Nothing good awaited. He had to get away.

"Travis! Come back!" He could hear Ms. Diane screaming. "Come back!" Too late. As he went deeper into the woods, her voice disappeared.

Chapter 6

This is stupid. This is stupid. This is stupid.

Words stung as branches smacked Travis with each step. His eyes adjusted to the darkness. He slowed to catch his breath.

The sounds of night echoed all around him. Bats, crickets, coyotes and the cold breeze ruffled the few, remaining leaves on trees. Although winter ended, the blossoming of spring had not yet begun.

He crouched, contemplating the best move. *Where should I go?* He shook his head, wiped sweat with his sleeve. *Turn around and go back to the house. Deal with the nagging, take the punishment. Go to sleep... This will blow over quick.*

But retreating to the house would lead to an even bigger mess, especially since he ran off. He didn't plan to *run away.* He wanted to *get away,* for a minute. After a brief break, he stood up and continued to meander.

Ooo! An owl flapped by Travis. He dropped to his feet and quickly raised his arms to cover his head. Rustling leaves creating a soft blanket on the cold ground.

This isn't worth it. Slowly standing to his feet, he inched forward. Then turned around, heading back to the house. With each move, a high-pitch, rattling sound increased.

Click-click-click.

Rattlesnake! Travis froze. The ground was too dark to tell where the snake was coiled. In front? Behind? Next to him? Which side is the snake on?

Why couldn't Diane or Craig pull up now? Being thrown and locked into a dark, dirty closet sucked. Eventually he'd get out. A rattlesnake ended in one way. Death.

"Craig, get out here!" Ms. Diane started to run to the barn, then stopped. She looked out in the woods. Her eyes adjusted to the darkness. She walked toward the end of the clearing of trees and shrubs. "Craig!" She looked back toward the rear door.

Mr. Craig ran out the back door. Fear and curiosity flooded his face. "What is it?"

"Travis, he ran out to the woods!" She jogged in the barn and fired up her four-wheeler.

Craig hustled into the house and returned to the porch with his hands loaded. He handed Ms. Diane a walkie-talkie and shotgun. "We need to watch out for bobcats. I don't think the black bears will be out yet. It's still too cold for them to come out of hibernation."

"Let's hope not," she called over the pulsing growl of their four-wheelers running. She drove out of the barn first and waited for Mr. Craig to pull up next to her. "Which way?"

He leaned over and cupped his hands. "I'll go right. You veer left."

Ms. Diane nodded and pointed back at the house.

"I left a radio inside." She saw two thumbs up from her husband and took off.

Yeeeeeen! Yeeean!

Mr. Craig and Ms. Diane rode separate paths on their unfenced property. Over roots, around trees and ponds, and under branches.

"I don't get why that boy ran off." Ms. Bridgette adjusted on the couch.

"How long are we gonna stay here?" Kelsey flopped onto a plush brown chair. The living room seemed empty. Lifeless without Ms. Diane's bubbly smile and Mr. Craig's occasional laugh.

Brooke sat next to her aunt, puzzled. Why was Travis mad at her? Why? She didn't do anything to him. It was Kelsey that had the nickname for Travis on the bus. She fidgeted on the oversized, beige couch.

It felt like hours. But the large grandfather clock never chimed.

Tick, tock. Tick, tock. The house was still, other than Kelsey's sighs, and Jon walking up and down the hall.

Chhh! Sudden static of the radio caused Brooke to jump.

"Diane, anything?" Mr. Craig barked over the radio. There was a pause for some time.

"I checked around the ponds. Didn't see anything. What about you?" She pulled her hair back and brushed spider webs from her arms.

"Nothing over here," he replied. "Jon, you okay at the house? Did he come back yet?" Mr. Craig rested a hand on his lap and held the two-way radio next to his ear.

"We're fine. He didn't come back yet." Ms. Bridgette checked the time on her phone.

"Diane, mark your location," Mr. Craig instructed. He pulled off his canvas bucket hat, wiped sweat beads from his forehead and sighed.

"Craig, I'm ready," she answered. "Go."

Then there was silence.

Brooke's mind wandered. How different was Travis' home life than her's had been? Both were bad. Living in suburban Mobile, Alabama sounded perfect, but inside those four walls she suffered physical and verbal abuse. It ended with her father beating Brooke and her mother one night, nearly killing her and taking her mother's life.

She lived with Kelsey and her aunt Ms. Bridgette in a single-wide trailer, just past the Mooring property on County Road 86. Living in rural Garden County had been as much a culture shock to her as it had been to Travis. But after living here since third grade, it felt like home.

She missed having her own space and the beach a mere thirty minutes away. But sharing a bedroom with Kelsey and living with Aunt Bridgette and their black lab, Susie, was much better than the violence she had survived.

"Anything on the radio yet?" Jon crept in the living room to check with Ms. Bridgette.

"No. Just had another check-in from Diane and Craig. Nothing." She sighed, and stroked Brooke's hair. Then glanced over at Kelsey, who'd given up scrolling through Instagram.

Kelsey didn't really care much for whole situation – the backpack, Travis running away. She didn't understand *why* Ms. Bridgette dragged Brooke and her to the Mooring's house after a grueling evening softball practice. What good was really going to come from seeing Travis after he threw Brooke's backpack out the window? And *why* did her mom make *her* apologize? All Kelsey was doing was defending Brooke.

"Hey Craig? Any luck?" Ms. Diane shouted. Within seconds there was a reply.

"Diane," Mr. Craig began. "Anything around you?"

"No," she said.

Another check-in. Time wasted. Sitting around waiting on a loser to come home. Kelsey could've gotten homework done. Relaxing at their home. Or doing something that she *wanted* to do instead of laying here, doing nothing.

"Mark your spot and let's keep moving," Mr. Craig answered. I'm going to start heading a little more north."

"Okay," she replied. "Hey, Bridgette, anything new? Any update?"

"No ma'am. He hasn't come back yet." She glared at Kelsey while replying to Ms. Diane.

"Timer set. Let's roll," Mr. Craig said.

Kelsey mouthed "What?" and readjusted herself on the chair. She didn't get why her mom insisted on bringing them over, especially after all that the three girls had been through. Brooke's past with her father, and the loss of her mom, Kelsey's aunt. Not to mention Kelsey's distrust of all boys because of her estranged father.

He used to come stumbling home at five or six in the morning from a late trip to visit the casinos. Sometimes Kelsey woke up to her parents arguing or hearing the door slam. Other times to the police banging on the door, responding to frantic 911 calls of her missing husband, only to find him drunk in his truck or on the porch.

Within a week of her sister's death, Ms. Bridgette had enough and filed for divorce. She kicked Kelsey's father out, vowing that he was never to come back there again.

Kelsey took her anger out on any guy she saw- whether it was male classmates, male teachers, or males she ran into. This included Jarel and now, especially Travis. If her own daddy was no good, why would some other boy?

"Why don't you guys get going? I'll listen for them." Jon picked up the radio from the coffee table and looked at the girls. Brooke, half asleep, rested her head on Ms. Bridgette's shoulder. Kelsey was curled up on Mr. Craig's recliner, next to her cell phone.

"Yeah, it's getting late. The girls are ready for bed. Tell them to call for help. It's dangerous out there in the woods for that boy."

"Yes ma'am. You're right, especially for a city boy."

"Wasn't too long ago when you were that boy! Looks like Diane and Craig did some good for you!" A weary smile grew onto his face.

Jon lowered his head. "Yes ma'am. Can't say how blessed I was."

Ms. Bridgette's words hung in the air as he stood in the empty Mooring's home.

"Craig," Ms. Diane began. "I'm calling. This is too long."

Thirty minutes for a lost boy on a cold night felt like an eternity. No answer. She dialed 911 on her phone.

"911, what's your emergency?" greeted the responder. Before Ms. Diane could reply she heard. The kind of sound that sent shivers up a mother's spine, the kind of cry that led to heart attacks.

"Ms. Diane! Help!" A depleted, desperate voice cried.

"This is 911, what's your emergency?" the responder repeated.

"Wait a minute..." Ms. Diane held the phone down to her chest. She hopped off her four wheeler, and studied the darkness. She wandered around, eyes scanning. "Travis?"

"Ms. Diane?" the responder asked. "You okay?"

"Hey, Pa…" Ms. Diane paused. "Send a deputy to my-"

"I'm over here." Travis' voice sounded desperate, pleading, begging for more than help. "Help. I got bit."

"Send an ambulance to my place! I gotta go!" Ms. Diane hung up. Her radio continued to call. But her attention was on finding where Travis' voice was coming from. Clutching the phone she looked around, peering through streaks of moonlight.

Covered in sweat, he sat leaned against a tree. Vine wrapped around his right leg above the knee with scratches across his arms. Even in the dark, she could see the loss of color in his face.

"Look out. I don't know where the snake went." He tried to yell but it was only a whisper.

"Do you remember how many times it bit you?" With no concern for her own safety, she rushed to Travis and placed his arm around her neck. Gently, she pulled him to his feet.

"Twice…" Travis winced. They slowly hobbled onto her ATV.

"Diane. Diane! Where you at?" he asked. An escalated level of panic crept into Mr. Craig's voice.

"Hold on!" She demanded, realizing that her husband was calling. She helped Travis climb atop the ATV.

"I found Travis! He got bit by a snake! I need to get him back to a main road now!" She looked around. Panic began to set in.

"How far you are from the highway? That's closer than riding back across the property."

Ms. Diane checked her surroundings. "Don't think I'm too far off. Maybe close to Baron Road."

"Go there. I'll call for a medic and deputies to be looking out."

Travis slouching, his motionless body in front of Ms. Diane as she navigated them through the woods to the nearest patch of clearing.

Ms. Diane drove through the wilderness as fast as she could without losing control of the ATV and Travis. They reached a clearing and found a paved road. Within seconds she saw a set of headlights. A spot light came on. Then a light bar flashing red and blue.

"Help is here," she whispered, struggling to catch her breath. Mr. Craig arrived a few minutes later as the ambulance pulled up. Travis was rushed to the hospital as Mr. Craig rode along. A deputy took Ms. Diane back to the house.

"Lord help us," Mr. Craig whispered. "This is gonna be a long spring."

Chapter 7

It took a few minutes for Travis' eyes to adjust. Cream-colored wallpaper sporadically imprinted with little pink flowers. A mix of natural light from a window as wide as the room and fluorescent lights above illuminated the scene.

He looked left, at the machine. Hoses, gadgets and sticky pads from the device connected to him. Then noticed he had company. He struggled to sit up.

"Relax," Lincoln said. "You took a really big dose of venom from that snake." Lincoln stopped typing on his phone and set it in his lap.

"Where am I?" Travis rubbed his eyes.

"DCH. Kid's ward. Best artwork of any hospital I've been to." Lincoln toyed with his phone. "Man, this game is so addicting! Asphault 8. You gotta try it."

Travis rolled his eyes. Then he turned over. His eyes stopped on the figure staring back at him.

"Oh yeah, Ms. Diane is here." He paused. "She's been here since you were brought to the hospital. Well, I've got to make a couple calls. Actually a couple *missed* calls." His attempt to lighten the mood fell flat. Lincoln never had a great sense of humor. As he walked out, he nodded at her and greeted a nurse.

Ms. Diane slid over to the chair by the bed. He stared ahead, unable to face her. After a few seconds she placed her hand on top of his. He didn't pull his hand away, but slowly brought his eyes to hers. Sadness masked her face. Similar to the look that Brooke had when her backpack went out the window.

Flashback to a distant memory. He remembered seeing a person look this sad, but not out of concern for him. He'd seen his mom look like this before; she would occasionally get this look when she wanted something. Something Travis couldn't give her.

Valentine's Day night four years ago, the sad look turned into a fierce fight. The yelling isn't what woke him up, though. No, it was the earth-shattering boom. A forceful wave of energy unlike anything Travis had ever felt. Harder than the deep *thud* when Uncle Eddy blocked his shot at the park. Scarier than when Travis tripped and landed hard on the outdoor courts at Smiley Court Apartment. Louder than the time Travis got knocked off his feet and slammed his head into the wall.

BOOM!

"Mo..." The word nearly slipped out of his mouth.

"Shh, just rest, T." The corners of her lips rose. Her eyes shined as she held his hand. His heart melted.

Travis couldn't remember the last time he heard that nickname. He was too weak to lash out, too emotionally spent and physically exhausted. There was only thing he could do. He cried.

A deep, lasting, relieving cry.

She wiped his tears. He wanted to pull her hand back and hold it. But it felt soft on his cheek as she tried to keep up with the flow of tears streaming. She smiled, biting back her own tears.

The ride back to the house was anything but quiet, although it was only the two of them. Within minutes of pulling out of the loop of the hospital, Travis had flipped through radio stations. He paused at 105.1 Jamz.

"Boy, please. This isn't music!" Ms. Diane shook her head. She started doing the *Hammer time* dance at one light, then followed it with the *Cabbage Patch* dance at the next. "Now *that* is moving! Not some *dabbing* and *Nae-Nae*!"

"Those are old moves! From the old days, before people drove cars," Travis blurted.

"Boy, we had cars *and* air conditioning in my day. We even had *cell phones*!"

"So what do you think about Brooke?" She didn't warm up to it. He wasn't even ready to talk about something as serious. Travis stared ahead at the road.

Their Ford Expedition was further down Interstate 20, clearing out from the hustle and bustle of city traffic. There was hardly any traffic ahead. The sun was shining, with the rays beaming down.

"She's cute, isn't she?" Ms. Diane smirked.

Rapidly, the temperature rose in the truck. Travis felt beads of sweat grew on his forehead. This was an unexpected twist. He was preparing for a defense of the incident on the bus, ready to rat about Kelsey punching him, and Brooke throwing pencils and pens at Jarel.

How did she even know that? I haven't said anything to anyone, including Jarel, about Brooke. She was cute, sweet, smart, and word is that she's an athlete.

"She's nice too." Ms. Diane adjusted her hands on the steering wheel. Travis opened his mouth but nothing came out.

"Do, you... agree?" She dragged it out, waiting for what seemed like an eternity for his reply.

"Yes, she is."

The silence after he spoke. He felt Ms. Diane was waiting for him to say more. He wanted to talk, but this topic created butterflies in his stomach.

"Relax, I won't say anything to Brooke, or Ms. Bridgette... or Kelsey!" She made a squishy face. Travis burst out in laughter. Not only did Ms. Diane jump, but Travis did too.

"My bad," he laughed.

"You better figure out a way to get on her good side if you want a chance with Brooke. Not to say that you should be worried about girls. The only girl you should be trying to please is *me!*"

She smiled at Travis, then jokingly batted her eyes. "*Worry about your books and pleasing your mom.*" He heard friends, like Jarel, mimic their fathers.

"Watch what Craig does when we get back. He's so romantic. He knows how to sweep me off my feet!" She placed a hand over her chest like her lungs were unexpectedly deflated.

"Mm hmm," Travis sarcastically replied. "Well, I did practice some of his tips on you." He quickly added, "Remember that moonlight ride that I took you on, with the four-wheeler?"

"Boy, I had you strapped onto the four-wheeler to keep from falling off. I guess it was so impressive that it took your breath away." She could hardly keep from laughing between words.

"What about when we shot hoops?" He was really trying. Like a true competitor, going from game to game, loss to loss, persistent that the next challenge would result in a win.

"I got tired of watching you jack up bricks, so I decided to show you how to shoot."

"Ms. Diane, did you play ball back in the day?" He realized that this was a no-win conversation. Then unintentionally changed the topic.

She smiled, reminiscing on games, practices, and trips. "Sure did."

"Pro?"

"No hon. There wasn't a WNBA or pro league in the U.S. back then. I played in college, won a couple rings. That's where Craig managed to sweep me off my feet." Ms. Diane still wanted to talk about Brooke.

Travis thought of the top women's basketball programs. *UConn, Stanford, South Carolina. What were the good teams back in the day? Tennessee, USC, Baylor?*

"And not at some uppity D1 school," she continued. "I played at North Dakota State, a D2 school. We were the cream of the crop back in my time. We won two championships while I was there, then two more after I graduated."

"What? I guess that explains why you shot so well."

The remainder of the trip was all about basketball – about how good Ms. Diane's team was and the Lady Buffalos domination of the early 1990s. She dazzled Travis with her knowledge of current and past NBA stars and facts.

Talk about an exciting car ride home. Did I say home? The word slipped through his thoughts.

Travis sat with angst getting ready for school the next day. He missed almost a week from the hospital stay and recovering at the house.

"Don't worry. Jarel will have your back tomorrow." Ms. Diane leaned against the doorway to his bedroom. She smiled.

"Me and Jarel only have three classes we have together." He looked forward, in a daze. "Anyway, it doesn't help when I see the girls at lunch."

"You already saw them, and scared them off. Stay away from Kelsey's backpack, and you'll be okay. And watch out for her right hand!"

"Come on, Mo…" Travis caught himself. This was the second time he almost slipped. Ms. Diane didn't even look like his mother, not one bit. No one looked like Cheryl Johns. Not Ms. Bermas and her nasty scowl, careless supervision, and negative treatment of Travis at the hands of the boys he lived with. Not Mrs. Virginia with her fake smile, empty, cold house and unattached method of talking at Travis instead of with him. Definitely not Ms. Diane. Aside from that moment in the hospital, with that look in her eyes, Travis had never thought of her as a mother. Not as if he really knew what moms are supposed to do.

The only thing he recalled that Ms. Diane and his mother had in common was blonde hair. Even that was different. His mother's hair was really brown with lots of blonde highlights while Ms. Diane's golden hair was highlighted with silver. *Grey hair definitely can't be a result of stress.* She smiled too much.

Including their hair, the two ladies were different in other ways. Ms. Diane was a morning person, and had routines. Chores, Sundays at church, and "family night" were all part of the new life Travis was forced to adjust. Travis' mother was never awake before the sun came up. He remembered getting himself dressed for school when Uncle Eddy was already gone for work.

Ms. Diane *always* smiled. Sometimes she'd just look at Travis and get a huge grin on her face, or saying something silly or small-talk with him or Jon or Craig that made her happy. Travis' mother was the total opposite—only one thing made his mother happy. Neither were good. The stench and the dreary look in her eyes when she was happy made Travis queasy. He couldn't understand how sniffing powder through rolled-up money was exciting.

People *loved* to be around Ms. Diane. If it was folks at church with what Travis referred to as "Sunday smiles" or folks at the shops around town, or at Raymond Blake Middle School. Even when they went to Tuscaloosa to the bigger stores, she managed to make friends with strangers. But it wasn't the same with Cheryl Johns. Random people entered their dingy apartment for one of two things. Private time or money. Even then they would fuss with her. There was always someone over arguing with her about something. Plus nightly arguments between Uncle Eddy and Travis' mom were stressful. He wanted to take Travis to a safe place and a job in Mobile, then Pensacola, then one time he mentioned Atlanta.

Atlanta. That was the end of talking. That was the eve of Valentine's Day.

"Shh, he's coming," Ms. Diane cheesed. "Watch him. Do this with Brooke!" She quickly glanced down the hall, then back to Travis, as if to seem surprised when Mr. Craig came around the corner.

"Hey Di." Mr. Craig walked around and looked into her eyes. "Are you almost done with Travis? I need to speak to him for a minute."

"Oh, yes. I'm done, dear." She smiled at him, like there was a twinkle in her eye. The look resembled the toddler song "Twinkle, Twinkle, Little Star."

"You sure? I don't want to rush you." He just looked at her. It didn't seem like anything special. Travis had no clue what she wanted him to watch Mr. Craig for.

"Yes. You go coach him up!" she said. She gently rubbed the back of his head before looking back at Travis and walking off.

Man, sometimes that lady is really cool. But sometimes she doesn't make any sense.

As she walked off, Mr. Craig looked back towards her. He then gave a childish wave in her direction.

Weird married-people stuff.

Mr. Craig's smile disappeared as he turned around toward Travis. He closed the door behind him and slowly sat in a chair by Travis' bed.

Good Cop disappeared. Time for Bad Cop to deliver the rest of the punishment. Now came the harsh part.

Chapter 8

The conversation went much smoother than Travis expected. The main issue was replacing Brooke's backpack. It'd be tough to locate the pink PB bag like the one she had. Travis and Mr. Craig climbed into his truck and began their backpack-hunting trip to town.

"Got any ideas where we should start?" Mr. Craig backed down the dirt driveway.

"Uh, I guess the mall." Travis buckled his seatbelt. *We are in for a long night.*

After spending hours roaming multiple Tuscaloosa malls, the two were exhausted. "Maybe we can try online?" Travis said He noted the unhappy look on Mr. Craig's tired face. "I'll try as soon as I get home." Mr. Craig reached for his cell phone.

Oops. The h word... home. He couldn't recall any time he slipped up and called a foster placement his *home.* He only referred to Smiley Court Apartments as *home.* But it existed no more. Cheryl Johns didn't exist. Nor did Uncle Eddy. Therefore, Travis thought *home* didn't exist anymore, nor would it ever.

Travis snapped back to reality as the truck turned around and headed towards a strip mall they just passed.

"Uh huh," Mr. Craig replied. "Okay, thanks Bridgette. We're going there now." He hung up and placed the phone in the center console. "There's a place up here where Bridgette bought the backpack." He scanned store and street signs.

Please let them have it. Travis's stomach churned at the image of Brooke sitting on the bus, staring after he threw her bag out the window. Her disbelief mixed with tears. He knew better. He'd do anything to make up for his actions.

Travis hopped out of the truck and sprinted into the store before Mr. Craig could unbuckle his seatbelt.

"PB backpacks?" He was out of breath after barging through the door. The question sounded more like a hopeful plea.

"The girl backpacks?" asked the cashier. Her face turned blank, seeming bewildered she replied. Then pointed. "Aisle eight." Mr. Craig entered a few seconds later.

Travis' eyes moved faster than he could read. He scanned the hanging bags once, twice. No PB teens or pink backpacks. *Doomed,* he sighed.

"Look." Mr. Craig pointed in front of Travis. "Pink bag, some girls on there… What are they playing? Is that volleyball?"

"Oh, that's it," Travis exclaimed. "No, that looks like a basketball goal and the net there." He held up the bright pink bag, then examined the design. "We got it!"

His smile vanished as he faced Mr. Craig.

"$42.99." He looked solemn.

Travis tried his best to sound hopeful. "I… uh, I guess I'll be working this off."

"On top of your punishment."

They walked to the register. Travis was back to what he did best, digging holes with people around him. Unlike the past, he was determined to find a way to solve this problem. And, he had the right people around him who'd have his back.

The next day Ms. Diane took Travis to school. She drove into the parking lot instead of the student drop-off lane. Red flags went up in Travis's head.

"We have a meeting with Dean Matts." She squinted, leaning forward to make sure her truck could fit into the narrow parking spot. "Oh, don't be so worried. The worst part already happened." He dropped his head as she patted his arm.

"Good morning. Come have a seat." Dean Matts ushered them to two seats across the table from Ms. Bridgette and Brooke. He was surprised to see everyone there for this unexpected conference.

Travis pulled the chair out and sat across from Brooke. He could hardly lift his head. He felt the weight of Ms. Bridgette's glare. But it was the sadness in Brooke's eyes that burdened him.

While Ms. Diane exchanged pleasantries with Ms. Bridgette, she gently wrapped her arm around Travis' back. He couldn't understand why she acted so friendly. *Ms. Bridgette is the enemy!*

He realized she was there to support him. She began to softly rub the back of his neck. He lifted his head. But he almost fell out of his seat when he heard Ms. Diane's reply to the recommendation to a five-day suspension off the bus.

"That's it?" Ms. Diane asked. She looked around the room, then at Travis. "I guess it'd be nice if we found a way to make it up to her, don't ya think?"

Dean Matts raised an eyebrow. "What do you have in mind?"

Travis mustered a nod. *What's she talking about? What else is can I do? I already got her a new backpack. Now I have to work off the cost.* Travis felt his anger build.

"We'll figure something out," she said while patting Travis's hand. His anger level dropped with each tap of her hand. It was as if she had superpowers.

Travis zoned in and out of the conversation, mostly thinking about Ms. Diane and Brooke. The mere presence of each provided motivation for him to want to do better.

While glancing at Ms. Diane, his mind flashbacked to last week in the hospital. He thought about seeing her eyes when he woke up, and accidently called her *Mom*. How warm and loving she had been to him, even when he didn't deserve it, when he tried to push her away. He couldn't understand why she cared for him. Foster parents didn't receive much money for taking in kids.

Travis periodically lifted his head and caught a glimpse of Brooke, wondering what he could do to make it up. He didn't really know much about her. *She was Kelsey's cousin and lived with her. What happened to her parents? Why doesn't she live with them? Are they alive?* For the first time, he was thinking about someone else.

"I will speak with Mrs. Rachel to make sure Travis and Brooke are separated on the bus," Dean Matts added. "How's that sound Brooke?"

"Good." Her voice was soft, hurt.

"Ms. Bridgette?" he continued.

"That's fine." Ms. Bridgette paused. "I saw her backpack when she got it back."

"Mm hmm," Dean Matts nodded. "It looked pretty beat up. Ms. Diane, I was under the impression that Travis was looking for a replacement, correct?"

"Yes, sir." Even when she was solemn she spoke with a delightful ring. "Craig and Travis went to town yesterday to find one." She frowned. "I believe it was similar to the other one. But in our haste this morning we forgot to grab it, right Travis?"

He nodded.

"We'll drop it off this afternoon, Bridgette. Or we'll be sure to bring it tomorrow morning when I bring Travis to school. Is that okay, Brooke? Or would you like me to run home and grab it now?" If she went home to get the backpack, she'd be late for work. Even if she was late, it probably wouldn't matter to anyone in Garden County. Everyone loved her so much, she could probably take candy from a baby and the *baby* wouldn't cry.

"*Brrring! Brrring!*"

"That's the bell for class," Dean Matts announced. "Ladies, anything else that you would like to address with the students here? If not, do you mind if I send them to class?"

"No, I don't have anything else to say." Ms. Bridgette glared at Travis.

"Same here," Ms. Diane replied. "Bridgette, you have my number. Just call and we can figure out the best time to get Brooke her new backpack."

"Sounds good," she answered.

Dean Matts looked at Brooke and Travis. "You can head to class. I'll see you at lunch."

The middle schoolers stood up simultaneously, rushing to leave the office. Travis hesitated at the door. He held it for Brooke and motioned for her to go first. Their first period class was in the same wing. But the tension led them to walk a couple feet apart, Brooke a few feet ahead of him.

"Hey, Br…" Travis wanted to say something meaningful. But he didn't want to sound like a wussy. He still had to regain a tough, stoic image after the hospital stay.

She turned her head to see Travis from the corner of her eye, pretending to glance at a poster. When she realized he was still behind her, she quickly turned forward.

Ugh, blew it. Just say something, man.

Nothing came out. Brooke entered her class. Travis continued to the next room.

"Where were you?" Jarel greeted. The simple answer was meeting with the dean. But the truth was thinking about Brooke. Travis' mind remained there for the next couple of days.

On the last day of his bus suspension, Travis sprinted to the blacktop at Raymond Blake Middle School. Ms. Diane dropped him off with enough time to play one or two games before class.

"Yo!" Jarel hollered as Travis flung his backpack to the fence. "You ready to hoop today?"

Travis nodded while stretching. The side effects of last week's stupid voyage in the woods wore off. His leg felt better and he was moving smoothly. *Ready to ball, baby!*

He stepped on the court, traded fist-bumps with Jarel and got ready to guard. This was it. Pure happiness for Travis. One thing he loved most about playing basketball is winning counted the most. It didn't matter who you were, where you lived, your past or what obstacle faced you after the game was done.

On the first play, Travis got beat on a backdoor cut. "My bad," Travis pounded his chest.

"You're good," Jarel said. "Get it back on the next play."

But the next play was just as bad. Travis's man pushed off just enough to get open on the wing. Travis staggered, then tried to recover his footing, but was too late. The offensive player caught the ball, but hesitated. He threw a wide-open jump shot that bounced off the rim.

Jaden hustled down the bouncing ball and Jarel set up the trio to execute a nice play. They evened the score. As Travis screened Jaden's man, the defender slipped and kicked him on his right leg where he was bitten by the snake.

"Ah!" Travis staggered to the ground. The defender fell over Travis as Jaden skipped to an easy lay-up.

"I think I'm done, man." Travis limped to the side after Jarel helped him up. Defeat and despair covered both boys' faces.

"I understand man," Jarel replied. "Rest up so we can get the dynasty going again."

"True." Travis fist-bumped Jarel. Another kid hopped onto the court to take his spot. The new team lost, seven to two.

"You wanna go by the cafeteria real quick?" Jarel said when the game was over.

"Sure." Travis was surprised by his lack of care about the game. *It's just pick-up ball. One loss doesn't break you, he remembered Jarel saying after their first time playing together.*

As they walked toward breakfast, Jarel continued talking about anything and everything under the sun: NBA season, spring break coming up, and riding the bus tomorrow…

"You nervous? Do you think Kelsey is gonna be ready to throw some hay-makers?"

"Man…" Travis shook his head.

"I'm joking, bruh." Jarel horse-played by bumping into Travis's arm.

"I'm sure it'll be fine. I just can't sit anywhere near Brooke."

"Okay. So you're trying to get me to move from my girl Kelsey?" Jarel frowned, then smirked. "Ah! Another joke, man. Kelsey and me aren't like that. I've known her so long… I just love messing with her."

Travis continued to check his surroundings. He hadn't faced either girl since the meeting in the dean's office.

Jarel's voice got real serious. "Brooke, even I don't mess with her. One, Kelsey gets serious about her and will split your jaw, like you found out. And two, that girl has been through a lot, man." He stopped and looked into Travis's eyes. "Not saying that you haven't, bruh. I mean, actually I don't really know much about you. But I do know what Brooke has been through. And that stuff ain't no joke." He opened the cafeteria doors.

Travis blurted. "What *stuff?*" He limped in behind his new best friend. The breakfast line was short. Students were throwing away their trash. The volume ear-shattering. Nonetheless, he only heard one sentence.

Jarel looked back. Solemn, serious. "How much time do you got?"

Chapter 9

Travis's breakfast consisted of a chicken biscuit, orange juice, and a history lesson on Brooke, Kelsey, and Ms. Bridgette. How the three ended up together as a forceful man-hating trio. Brooke was the least aggressive of the three, although she survived the worst of their experiences.

"So that's how Brooke ended up living with Kelsey and her mom, Ms. Bridgette. Crazy, huh?" Jarel threw out his trash.

Man, I have a lot in common with Brooke than I thought. All this time I thought she was a rural, cocoa brown cutie with curly hair that loves softball. He followed Jarel to class.

The next two days on the bus, the girls ignored Travis. Mrs. Rachel was the opposite, she watched him as much as she watched the road.

As Brooke and Kelsey walked by, Travis grew a goofy smile on his face in an effort to get at least a glance or a smirk from Brooke. Internally, he strained to say 'Hello' but could hardly get a sound out as she passed his new assigned seat on the bus.

"You alright?" Jarel sat up.

"Yeah," Travis said. "I'm good. Why?"

"Uh, well you're grinning real hard at Brooke." Jarel leaned back and shook his head. Then sat up to whisper. "Keep that up and Kelsey will take care of your smile." Travis didn't realize how obvious he was to everyone else on the bus.

"You need to face forward!" Mrs. Rachel scowled.

Travis's eyes stopped following Brooke. He straightened up.

"Take it easy man," Jarel whispered. "You'll get your chance to make it up to her. You got her a new backpack?"

"Yeah," Travis answered.

"Nice, man. I'm surprised you could find one."

"Me too..." Travis was busy scheming about how he could ease himself near Brooke's seat to begin earning her trust in fifth period class. Jarel continued to blab about the middle school's summer basketball team. He slowly began recruiting Travis, promising how great life and basketball could be in Garden County for the duo.

"Travis, are you lost?" Mrs. Ranson's hands rested on hips, eyes piercing his soul. In class, he stealthily attempted to switch seats by the door to sit one chair ahead of Brooke.

"Oh, no." He hesitated, trying to think of a good excuse. "I figured sitting up front would help me pay attention more." He pulled his math workbook from the backpack.

"Doing your homework would be a good starting point," she barked. Then motioned for him to move back to his old desk. "I'm not sure what you did at your old school, but it doesn't work like that around here. Next time, Dean Matts will help you understand."

Travis tried to seem calm as he collected his belongings and shuffled to the back of the room. As he flopped into his seat, Brooke glanced over. When she realized he noticed, she quickly looked away.

Yes! At least I got her attention, finally, he thought. A smirk came upon his face but then disappeared. *Maybe she was wondering why I tried to sit near her. Maybe she thinks I just care about school? Or maybe she is wondering why I keep trying to break the rules.*

Jaden tapped his shoulder. "You got a pencil I can borrow?"

"Yeah," Travis whispered as he dug into his backpack.

"Oh," Mrs. Ranson jumped. "So now you want to just talk and play in your backpack? Do whatever you want in class? You can go to Dean Matts's office and have a talk with him!"

"But I was getting a pencil for Jaden," Travis pleaded.

"Mrs. Ranson," Jaden began. "I asked him for…"

"Hush!" she snapped. "Unless you'd like to be part of the 'misery loves company' party. Mr. Mitchell, go tell your lame story to Dean Matts!" She slammed a yellow slip of paper on the corner of her table.

"I'll find out what your assignment is. You'll spend the remainder of fifth period in the class next door." Dean Matts picked up his office phone and dialed a number. He didn't seem as upset as Travis expected.

He looked around. This was the first time he noticed a poster. Huge black letters on a white backing with black frame. *Don't Quit. Why aren't all the letters shaded in?*

After a second it hit him. He realized that giving up on Brooke, Jarel, the Moorings, and his hope of finding a 'forever home' was at stake. Quitting, not trying his best to right the wrongs and live a new life would keep him from reaching any dream he had.

He was responsible for his future. Blaming his deceased mother for her failures and the short-coming of the other foster parents he had wouldn't solve his problems.

DON'T QUIT

"One question, what seat were you at?" He waited for an answer. Then replied as a lady's voice screeched *Hello?*

"Hey, it's Matts. What pages does Travis need to complete? Uh huh, okay. Thanks." He closed his eyes as if he was balancing between meditation and frustration. "Yes, okay. Yup. Will do."

He hung up the phone and sighed, or possibly prayed. He spoke. "Do me a favor. Stop getting kicked out of Mrs. Ranson's class."

Everyone was tired from a night of games and family time and stuffed from snacking the night before. Typical Saturday morning at the Mooring's home. But it didn't stop Ms. Diane from concocting a creative breakfast to start the day.

She made biscuits and mixed fruit for Mr. Craig and Travis. By 8:30, the two were roaming the property, and headed for the barn. Mr. Craig pushed one door open and motioned for Travis to do the same with the other door.

Whew, no bags of concrete mix, he thought. For the past week, Ms. Diane mentioned paving the dirt court outside next to the barn. *I'm not doing all that work!*

"There's some land out back that we're going to clear." Mr. Craig shuffled around some tools. The dimly lit barn was packed full of tools. Chainsaws, shovels, air compressors, and gas tanks.

"With what?" Travis asked.

"Well," Mr. Craig huffed and puffed. "I'm using the backhoe. You grab the smaller roots and limbs." He turned around. "Just look out for any soft spots."

"How much land are we going to clear?" Travis inquired. He began thinking of how much work and time he would have to spend outside.

"As much as we can clear in a day," Mr. Craig smiled. "If we don't finish, we'll get back at it next week. Find Jon, ask if he is coming out to help."

Travis dragged his feet outside the barn and saw Jon jogging down the steps.

"Hey, are you coming to help?" Travis asked.

"Help you do what?" Jon questioned.

"Going to clear land." Travis kicked a loose rock by his foot.

"Eh, I'll pass. I'm gonna stay inside and help Ms. Diane." Jon began to head back inside the house. "Mr. Craig, you want my help or not? I was gonna run some errands with Ms. Diane."

"That's fine," he replied, then reappeared with two handfuls of tools. "I'll get your help another weekend."

Jon turned to Travis and grinned. Then he hustled into the house.

"What a beautiful day to be outside!" Mr. Craig leaned a shovel and iron rake into Travis' chest. He went back into the barn and fired up the backhoe. Within a few minutes, he returned riding the twenty-three foot machine.

"Follow me," Mr. Craig yelled as he turned the corner from the barn.

Travis felt he had no choice but to comply. He'd rather spend the day shooting, passing and working on his skills on the basketball court than clearing land.

"If we make a good amount of progress, I'll let you drive the backhoe," Mr. Craig smiled. "A lot of fun once you get the hang of it."

Travis was intrigued by the opportunity to do something new. Mr. Craig trusted him enough to operate expensive machinery. Travis perked up and moved with some energy.

The two worked all morning. The area was larger than the minuscule dirt court. Travis tirelessly pulled shallow roots and carried small limbs. Sweat dripped down his neck and back. He didn't sweat this much playing basketball. His hands weren't as sore, either.

Mr. Craig spent most of the time giving commands. "Move back! Watch your step! Push it onto the bucket!" He operated the backhoe smoothly. Turning, moving sideways, lifting and dropping loads. Travis yearned to learn how to work the machine as gracefully.

Eventually, the backhoe chewed up more land than could be cleared. Mr. Craig shut off the backhoe and began shoveling, raking and flattening land with him. "Doesn't have to be perfect," he said, moving faster than Travis. "Just make sure there's no big, uneven spots where someone can trip."

Ms. Diane called the two up to the porch. Sandwiches, bananas, and two Gatorade bottles waited on the table.

"Don't eat too quickly," Mr. Craig warned. He took another bite of his sandwich and chewed slowly. "You'll be throwing up all over that shovel and rake." Travis looked away, then continued scarfing down his sandwich before grabbing a second. He was hungry and exhausted. He finished two sandwiches and a banana before Mr. Craig finished his sandwich.

Mr. Craig seemed in no hurry to get back out in the sun. "We need to let the food digest if we're gonna be any good out there. Second half of the day is always rougher than the first." The timer rang on his phone. He slowly sat up and stretched. Then stood up. "Time to get back on it."

Travis hurried to get out there and complete the project. *The quicker we start, the quicker we finish.* As he watched Mr. Craig, he thought about Brooke, basketball, and the future.

Soon after getting back to work, Travis felt a painful cramp in his side. It felt as if someone slapped his side. He tried to work through it. A few minutes later, he slouched over and held his stomach. The pain was unbearable. An irritating tingle crawled through his body.

Mr. Craig sighed, then drove the machine back to the barn. He motioned for Travis to bring the tools inside. Then shook his head.

"Go sit on the steps on the back porch for a minute." Mr. Craig didn't seem sympathetic. But Travis realized he should've taken the advice and gone easy on lunch.

He spit up quarts of blue fluid. *Gatorade. It doesn't feel as good coming out as it did going down. That was stupid. I gotta smarten up.* He threw up more and the pain of an empty stomach grew.

On the bus ride Monday morning, Travis managed to move back one row to join Jarel in Seat 12. The girls were behind them discussing their Spring Break plans next week.

"So the tournament was cancelled?" Brooke asked.

"Yup." Kelsey continued texting a Lady Tiger softball player. "They're going to a different tournament somewhere in Atlanta."

"Ah, Atlanta," Jarel interrupted. "Chocolate City. Home of the Brave, well, Braves. The high, flying 28-to-3 Falcons. The Hawks. Birds of prey!"

"What are you doing?" Kelsey was irritated by Jarel's shenanigans.

"But, the Big Easy is the place for me," he smiled, ignoring her warning. He cupped his hands together, then began mocking the sound of a pelican.

"You're crazy," Brooke laughed.

"He's about to get knocked out," Kelsey cautioned. Her fists clenched.

"Chill, girl. That's the sound of a pelican. Y'all need an edu-ma-cation!" Jarel's favorite, made-up word. "You haven't heard of the Pelicans? *The Brow, Bayou Block Party, Nawlins Negator?*"

"No, no, and NO! What are you saying? Speak English, boy!" Kelsey barked.

Jarel shook his head, then directed Travis. "Help these poor girls out, man."

"He's talking about Anthony Davis," Travis laughed. "Davis plays for the New Orleans Pelicans. NBA team."

"Duh, I'm not dumb." Kelsey snapped. She seemed ready to jump over the seat and pound his face in. "Maybe you can help us find a backpack for them. We *know* basketball."

"Oh, my bad. I just didn't..."

"Think," Kelsey finished his sentence.

"They don't have a WNBA team, right?" Brooke asked. She tried to keep the conversation going, spinning away from her cousin's volatile antics.

"No, I don't think so," Jarel stated. "Hey, what are you doing for Spring Break, Travis."

He looked around, unsure. Ms. Diane talked about going to a couple different places but it'd be a surprise. She said it may be the two of them if Jon did well in district weight-lifting tournament this last week of school.

The conversation fluttered, as did another opportunity for Travis to make some progress with Brooke.

There's always tomorrow, he thought. *But for how long?* He didn't know how long he'd be with the Moorings, or how many strikes he had left to get on Brooke's good side.

Surprises weren't something that Travis looked forward to. *Surprise, your mom's dead… and your uncle. Surprise, you're getting moved to a new home. Surprise, you're suspended.*

Maybe Ms. Diane could live up to her reputation. Maybe she had something special up her sleeve.

Although he was excited to have a break from school, he couldn't get worked up over this mystery spring break trip. *Don't get your hopes up. You know better.*

Chapter 10

The boys climbed onto the bus, ready for Spring Break to begin. "What's the plan for tonight? Four-wheeling? Clearing land? Game night?" Jarel joked. He was spending the night with Travis at the Moorings' home.

"Not sure, man." Travis ignored the lame humor. "We might get dragged back to school for the softball game tonight. Ms. Diane made us go to a game last week."

"Yeah, but we'll be at the high school," Jarel answered. "In a year we'll be preparing to dominate on the hardwood! A couple trips to the Final Four, win some state championships."

"First let's see if you can survive the night with the Moorings." Travis rolled his eyes.

"Man, you gotta set some goals, and dream. It all begins this summer!"

"If you're going to spend the whole night talking about the future, you better find a ride home. I want to enjoy this break." They hopped off the bus and walked down the dirt road leading to the Moorings' home. Ms. Diane's Expedition slowed next to them. "See y'all at the house," she waved and kept going.

"That's cold man. She could've given us a ride," Jarel said.

"Hah!" Travis laughed. "Man, you've got a long night ahead of you!"

After splitting a pizza and wins in two games on NBA 2K, it was time to go to the softball game at Garden County High School. During the whole car ride, Jarel talked about how he played with the New Orleans Pelicans to defeat Travis's Golden State Warriors.

"I know *how* I beat you, but I'm a little shocked I beat you *so badly!*" Jarel said.

"What was the score?" Mr. Craig asked.

"Oh man, I think 93-90."

"So you won by three. What'd Travis win by?" Jon continued texting but chimed in.

"I won the second game by 21... after Jarel wanted to quit when I was up 14-2," Travis added, smirking.

"Home court advantage," he argued.

"Jarel," Ms. Diane began. "I didn't realize you talked so much. How do you avoid Dean Matts's office?"

"It's simple, Ms. Diane. Since I can't talk *in* class, I have to get it out when I'm *not* in class!"

"Pretend you're in class when we drive back home," Mr. Craig said. The truck pulled into a grassy lot.

Everyone scattered once they entered the gate. Ms. Diane towards Ms. Bridgette. Mr. Craig sat with some of the other fathers, uncles and alumni. Jon went to the student section with his friends. The game had just begun. Stadium lights shone bright as the sun disappeared. Popcorn and boiled peanuts could be smelled for miles.

Travis and Jarel walked to the far end beyond the bleachers. They walked past a few Hawe County fans dressed in black and gold.

"You see the girls over there?" Travis asked. He leaned on the first base fence line.

"What are you talking about? It's all girls here," Jarel stated. "Can't believe we got dragged out here. Our girls are gonna get waxed."

"Brooke and Kelsey. Do they even play?"

"I don't know, man. I can't remember the last softball game I've been to. I think they're player-managers, on the team to help out and stuff."

"What?"

"They're good, but they don't play high school. They play on a travel team out of Tuscaloosa during the summer and fall. But they will definitely be balling out here next year."

"Oh, okay. What position do they play?"

"Kelsey plays first base and pitcher. And I hear Brooke is at shortstop and outfield. She's got wheels. She can outrun most boys in the county."

"Like you," Travis laughed.

"Ah... I bet you wish she was chasing you!"

Travis paused. "I'm elusive on the court. That's why you *always* want me on your team!"

"I want you on my team because you were the new kid and I didn't want to hurt your feelings or break your ankles."

Travis gave up. It was pointless to keep talking trash with Jarel. He played like Kyrie Irving but talked trash like Kevin Garnett. They spent the evening talking about the NBA season.

After the game, the boys returned home to play more NBA 2K. They eventually fell asleep around 3AM, watching game highlights.

The next morning began with a loud wake-up call. Ms. Diane had breakfast ready. Mr. Craig reminded Travis that he still had a half day of work to make up for.

"What time is it?" Travis groaned. He stumbled down the hall.

"Just after eight." Ms. Diane placed a stack of fresh pancakes on the table. "But you better get moving. Mr. Craig is waiting. He said y'all are gonna level the ground you cleared last week." She came back with a carton of orange juice. "Jarel, your mom will be here soon."

So much for an exciting start to spring break, Travis thought.

As the Moorings returned from church Sunday afternoon, Lincoln pulled in the driveway. Travis was thrilled to tell him about the upcoming four-day trip to Atlanta for Spring Break.

"Wow, that'll be a lot of fun!" Lincoln said. "What are you gonna do there?" The conversation continued from the front door, down the hall and into the living room. It'd been awhile since the two had something *positive* to talk about.

"Oh man," Travis sighed. He tried to recollect the places that Ms. Diane mentioned. "There's a lot to do! The College Football Hall of Fame, a news station, Dr. King's museum, Coca-Cola factory, and Georgia Aquarium. What else are we doing?"

They sat down at the living room. Travis remembered the Warriors had an afternoon game against the Memphis Grizzlies. He thought about turning the TV on, but wanted to talk about his trip.

Lincoln sprawled across the brown loveseat. He seemed more comfortable in the Mooring's house than ever before at a foster home. Shoes kicked off, legs crossed and propped up, head resting on the opposite arm rest. He was preparing for a Sunday nap rather than the usual check-in appointment. A sudden scent of fresh, baked chicken engulfed the house.

"That sounds about right." Ms. Diane hollered as she pulled out a plate for Lincoln. "Jon and Craig won't be able to go. Jon qualified for the state weightlifting tournament on Monday."

"Wow, that's great! Jon is will be a senior next year, correct?" Lincoln asked.

"Yes, sir," Ms. Diane smiled proudly. "Then my baby will be off to college!" She waved for the family to join her at the table.

The spread across the large, oak table was magnificent. A scene that didn't take long for Travis to get used to. Baked chicken, collard greens, corn bread, mac and cheese. Today's dessert was Monkey Banana Cream Pie.

"Then you guys will be stuck with me!" Travis said, without thinking. Slowly, he sat down. *That means that I'd be living with them, permanently. They all definitely heard me.*

He looked around, thinking of a way to backtrack his comment. "I mean, possibly. Have you guys ever *had* an empty house?"

This is awkward. Did Ms. Diane and Mr. Craig even have any kids of their own? Was Jon the only kid they adopted?

He was quiet during dinner. His eyes quickly glanced at five pictures on the wall. The last photo was of Travis playing basketball. Someone snagged a nice photo while he was soaring in the air, taking a jump shot. Between regretting his stupid comment earlier, he wondered who the other four boys were. Lincoln, Jon, Ms. Diane and Mr. Craig discussed weightlifting, scholarships, and college.

I've never said anything like that before.

"Travis, Travis," Ms. Diane gently nudged. "Can you pass the greens?" She smiled.

How could you not want to be around her? I mean, this lady really is the nicest person in the world. He passed the greens. *If it's too good to be true, then maybe it is. This trip would be a good chance to test her. I'll see if she's really that nice.*

Travis rolled over, taking a break from reading a *Sports Illustrated* story about Giannis Antetokounmpo's life, growing up in poverty in a violent country. He wondered if his situation, without a real home, compared to Giannis's struggles. Laying on his back, he closed his eyes. *At least Giannis had parents that wanted him.*

Knock, knock. Before he could reply, the bedroom door creaked open.

"Hey, honey. We'd like to talk to you." Ms. Diane walked in first, her face was solemn. Mr. Craig sat on a desk chair, slightly facing Travis. They looked at each other, telepathically having a cryptic conversation.

"Okay," he said as nonchalantly as he could muster. His mind raced. *I wonder if Lincoln told Mo- Ms. Diane that she can't take me out of state for our trip. Maybe it's my last week living here.*

"We have really love having you here and love you."

Blah, blah, blah. Just get to the bottom line. He sat up, then rested his head on his hands.

"We really loved having you here. We love you so much, and you add to our home. We feel complete with you here."

Thump, thump. Thump, thump. Travis's heart beat faster and faster.

"We would like you to live here, permanently. We want to adopt you." Ms. Diane finally smiled. Tears rolled down her cheeks.

And Travis's, too.

Chapter 11

"Get up!" Ms. Diane gently pushed Travis with one arm while exiting the highway.

"Where are we?" Travis rubbed his eyes.

"We're stopping for some coffee in Birmingham. Come on, slow poke! I wanna take some pictures here."

"Of what?"

"Oh Lord, we got some learning to do. Sixteenth Street Baptist Church." She hopped out of the truck while Travis struggled with his seatbelt.

"What?"

"Haven't you heard of the church bombing? All those years in Alabama schools and you haven't learned about your own state history." She shook her head. Then headed towards a huge stairway of a large brick building. Tears rolled down her cheeks.

Travis caught up, then rested his arm on her neck.

"I'm okay," she sniffled. "It's so sad. Those girls just wanted to be at church."

They spent an hour walking around, reading signs and learning about the four girls. Travis learned about the protest, the Selma Bridge march, and the bus boycotts. Slowly, they walked back to the Expedition, and found a coffee shop before getting back on I-20.

"Get used to it, Travis. I'll probably cry quite a bit during this trip." Ms. Diane tried to laugh.

"Why? Do you want to cry? Why would you want to go to sad places?"

"Well, I love history." Traffic picked up as they reached Douglasville, Georgia. "And unfortunately, a lot of sites show the painful scars of what hate has done."

Travis thought about his own history. He hated living in the past. He did not want to relive that pain and misery. *That's dumb.*

"I don't get it."

"How much do you know about Brooke and Kelsey?"

"A little bit. Jarel told me about Ms. Bridgette's ex-husband. Something happened to Brooke's parents. That's why she lives with Kelsey and her aunt."

"So you know Kelsey has a reason not to like you, much less any guy."

"Yup, I found out the hard way."

"After Brooke threw pencils at you? Or after you threw her backpack out the window?"

"Both!" Travis rubbed his jaw. "I really learned."

"So, no matter how nice you, or Jarel, or Mr. Craig are to them, do you think the girls are wrong not to trust you all?"

"Yes. I understand why they're hesitant with me, but with Jarel and Mr. Craig. Those guys are nice and caring, even though Jarel can be a bit talkative."

"So you're saying that the girls should forget about their past and trust guys. Forget about what they have experienced?"

"Yes! I've been trying to be nice since I've been back. But the girls don't buy it."

"Mm… hmm." She sighed loud enough for Travis to hear, but her tone seemed to indicate there was more.

"What's that for?" he pressed.

"Me? Oh, nothing." She looked forward at the road, trying to suppress a smile.

"Well, you're trying to make a point against my argument about the girls, about letting go of the past to..."

He paused, realizing what he said. He was sitting with a lady who wanted to adopt him, to care and love him for the rest of his life.

"Is that what this trip is about?" He dropped his head, thinking he knew what was next.

"Heavens no, I love history. The College Football Hall of Fame is about you. Harrell's Chicken and Ice Bar is kind of about you. Most of the trip is about me!" She smiled. "Remember? I love history. I almost became a social studies teacher. Didn't you know that?"

They continued the trip into downtown Atlanta in silence until they arrived. Lunch time was approaching, but the excitement of a new, big city created a different hunger, to explore the town.

They pulled into a parking garage. Then crossed a skyline bridge while walking out. It gave Travis a beautiful view of the Mercedes Benz Stadium.

"Wow!" Travis exclaimed.

"We got some better things to see than that!" Ms. Diane smiled. They headed into the CNN Center where Travis was able to test his skills as a broadcaster.

"Not bad!" Ms. Diane complimented. Travis rejoined her as they continued the tour.

After spending about an hour on the CNN tour, the two stopped at a fast food restaurant to grab lunch. Then headed to the NCAA College Football Hall of Fame museum.

"Man, Mr. Craig would've loved this place!" Travis cried.

At the NCAA College Football Hall of Fame, Travis had fun doing the Game Day experience. He predicted the Gators would upset Alabama. He was impressed with how well Ms. Diane could throw and kick on the college football field experience.

"All this yucky history stuff!" Ms. Diane commented while they toured the top floor.

Travis smiled. *Maybe history wasn't too bad, but it depended on what side you were on.*

"Ah, it's okay. Something to learn from. What's next?"

"The last site for today is the Center of Civil and Human Rights. There are some really neat things to see inside. It's right around the corner."

They continued walking. There were other options. Coca-Cola experience, the Georgia Aquarium. *Why go to something so serious?*

"Wow!" Travis's jaw dropped at the sight of the huge mural painted on the lobby wall. Sunlight shone through, helping clarify the contrast of scenes and colors on the drawing.

"Impressive, huh? Let's see what else is in here." Ms. Diane grabbed Travis's hand and charged ahead. He was disgusted. He wondered what his life would be like during segregation. Without his friends. No Jarel or Jaden. Would Brooke be alive? No Moorings.

"Oh, let's try this." Ms. Diane led Travis to the back of a long line.

"Don't you see how long the line is?"

"That must mean it's worth the wait!"

Must be 13 years or older.

13? You don't even go anywhere, he thought. While standing in line, he looked around. The two of them were the only white people in line. But he didn't think much of it. *Reminds me of Garden County.*

"Ready?" Ms. Diane checked with Travis. "This may be a bit intense."

"I'll be fine." He'd survived neglect, losing his mom, beatings and insults from the K-brothers. He could handle this two-minute sound booth. He sat on the barstool, put the headphones over his ears and rested his palms on the marked handprints. The last step included closing your eyes and listen.

He immediately was bomb-barded with yelling, screaming, and negative words shouted into his ears. One second, it felt like a man was standing on his left. A split-second later, another voice could be heard on his right. Then he heard glass shatter.

Kshhhhkshkshsh! He flung the headphones off. Then looked over to see Ms. Diane still listening, tears flowing.

An internally, dark cloud followed them through the rest of the exhibit. They saw a replica of the 16th Street Baptist Church. Then a scene of the balcony of the Lorraine Hotel where Dr. King was fatally shot.

When they reached the top floor when Travis finally spoke.

"I didn't realize this was happening all over the world," he whispered. His voice was hoarse. "Children and women are still suffering in Europe, Africa and Asia."

"Yup. There's always someone that has it worse," Ms. Diane replied.

By the time they left, Travis felt his stomach rumble. Ms. Diane heard, too. They walked back to the Expedition and turned the air conditioner up. Warm weather was settling in.

"Don't worry! We're off to dinner! Have you had chicken and waffles yet?"

"I remember chicken and grits. My uncle took me to a cool breakfast place. He was fun. He wanted to move to Atlanta."

"Really? Why?"

"I don't know. I guess for a job or more to do. Not too much to do in Alabama, he said."

The Expedition turned onto Auburn Avenue, then slowed by Ebenezer Baptist Church on one side and a museum on the left. Ms. Diane pointed at an eternal flame. They finally parked and walked into a restaurant.

Travis was overwhelmed by music, conversation and the smell of cooked food. Old school hip-hop blared through overhead speakers. Classic songs by Notorious B.I.G. and Outkast were the most familiar artists to the youngster. He looked around while they waited at a table. Paintings and murals of legendary civil rights members covered the walls.

Within minutes the two were scarfing down chicken and waffles with a side of collard greens. Ms. Diane's drink of choice was sweet tea. Travis preferred orange soda. With bellies full, they headed back to their hotel suite to rest for another day in town.

The next day, they returned to Auburn Avenue and toured the Martin Luther King Museum and Ebenezer Baptist Church. Travis ventured upstairs through a narrow stairway. It opened to maroon carpet and dark oak pews, which provided a grand view of the auditorium below. Golden pipes mirrored a large pulpit of famous Sunday sermons and community meetings. After sitting near the railing for a few minutes, Ms. Diane quietly walked out. Her head low, and a tissue close to wipe wet cheeks. Travis thought she looked somber. He quickly followed.

The duo walked past the memorial, down the street to see Dr. King's birthplace. The yellow two-story home, with brown wood trim imprinted a shadow on the well-maintained lawn.

Historical signs bordered the sidewalk. One street marker told of the first desegregated firehouses in Atlanta. Travis was amazed at how much there was to see and learn.

"This is better than class," he said. "Why don't they teach us about this stuff in school?"

"Good question," she said.

They took pictures: inside the museum, the memorial pool, and in front of 501 Auburn Avenue. For lunch, they ate pulled-pork barbeque with crisp, wedge-cut French fries. Then returned to their hotel suite.

"Rest up. We're doing something really fun this evening." Ms. Diane kicked off her shoes.

"Hurry up. Don't forget your hoodie." Ms. Diane rushed Travis while racing to the elevator. "We have to make sure we can get a good parking spot or we'll be late."

So far everything on the trip was great. There was no way she can keep this up. A light breeze crept into the evening. *What do I need to bring my hoodie for? It isn't that cold.*

"I need to trust you to hold onto something very important. Pull down the visor." She turned to Travis as they began switching lanes on I-285.

He complied. Two tickets dropped into his lap.

Atlanta Hawks' game. Tonight. He examined the tickets closer. They were playing against the Golden State Warriors. His first NBA game and he got to watch his favorite team play.

"What! How'd you know?" He hopped in his seat as if tacks were underneath. "Thank you!"

Travis was mesmerized. The pyrotechnics, before and during the game. A suddenly pitch black court, before laser red and yellow lights showed graphics on the court for player introductions. Booming music. Lit tiles on the court, shattering glass, and the hawk. Before tip-off, he asked Ms. Diane to take a picture with him. The court in the background, two huge smiles – a perfect photo. They feasted at a Chick-Fil-A booth with eight-dollar sandwiches during the game.

The game was thrilling. Back-and-forth. Slam dunks, alley-oops and three-pointers. Momentum swings, emotional rants from players. A mix of cheers and boos echoed the flow of the game. Ultimately, the Warriors won 114-109. Stephen Curry led the team with 38 points.

Travis's favorite play occurred during a big scoring run for Golden State. After a steal, Draymond Green sped down court and passed the ball to Klay Thompson. He knocked down a corner shot as two defenders sprinted to him.

Travis and Ms. Diane took their time leaving the Philips Arena. They enjoyed the monuments and banners from the late 1950's. Travis posed by the mural of Hawks' wings for fans to take pictures.

On their last day of vacation, they chose a late breakfast in the hotel. Travis enjoyed a whopping plate of French toast dripping with syrup, bacon, and fruit. Ms. Diane had a modest meal of cereal, fruit, and one more surprise.

"Aren't Brooke and Kelsey here for a softball tournament?" she asked.

"Oh yeah! They're playing here. Maybe we could see a game before we leave?" Travis tried to lower the level of excitement in his voice.

"I'll call Bridgette and see," Ms. Diane said. She quickly picked up her phone and dialed. "Hey, girl... Yes, what time is the game? ... Y'all are headed there now? ... Okay... Yes, Mhmm... Send the address.... Thanks! ... See you soon!"

Travis gobbled the remainder of his food and rushed Ms. Diane to quickly finish her meal. The two returned to their suite, packed their suitcases, and prepared to check-out.

As they walked into the sports complex, Ms. Diane and Travis searched for Field #3 where the girls were playing.

Travis spotted Brooke long before the rest of the team. He could tell from behind. A red and yellow hair bow held her curls. Almost on cue, she turned.

He smiled, another cheesy grin, like he had on the bus. Brooke grinned back and waved. Kelsey turned around, then squinted her eyes at him.

Yes, she finally smiled, Travis thought. *Progress!*

Chapter 12

"What's up, man?" Jarel greeted Travis as he slid over to his seat on the bus.

"Hey man," Travis said quietly, exhausted. His mind was still racing 100 miles per hour. Ms. Diane and Mr. Craig adopting him, seeing Brooke in Atlanta, the trip. He couldn't focus.

Jarel placed his backpack on the floor. "Yo, New Orleans was off the chain! What'd you do? And please don't say you stayed in town. If so, I hope you worked on your defense, because you were struggling last time."

Travis frowned. "What'd you do in New Orleans?"

"We did a lot of stuff. My uncle took me to a parade, we went to a Pelicans game, and I ate a bunch of jambalaya!" He turned around. "What's up, girls? I heard you went to Atlanta."

Kelsey rolled her eyes, then looked out the window. She ignored him, as usual.

"It was good. We went 2-2," Brooke said. She looked at Travis. The corners of her mouth turned upward.

"Oh, I see that smile," Jarel blurted. "You met some good-looking, swaggy fella up there!"

"Boy, please. No one has time for that or you. Turn around and shut up!" Kelsey barked.

"Wow... looks like the beast didn't get enough sleep last night." He turned to face forward.

"Haha," Brooke busted out. "I'm sorry, I'm sorry, Kelsey!" Her continuous laughter encouraged Jarel to continue with his jokes.

Travis chuckled and shook his head. *As long as she hits Jarel and not me.*

"Okay! Man, let's go to the court when we get to school. We gotta get back to balling on these folks!" Jarel pretended to shoot a jump shot. "I'm gonna ball like my boy AD!"

"AD is seven feet tall," Kelsey interrupted. "You're more like, seven *inches* small."

"Bahahaha!" Brooke continued giggling at Jarel's joke. But Kelsey's comeback was good.

The more Brooke chuckled, the more Travis smiled. When she laughed from her belly, the sound was contagious enough to fill the bus. Unfortunately other students, or the bus driver didn't appreciate the noise from middle schoolers.

"Hey, bring it down," Mrs. Rachel demanded.

"My bad. I told Kelsey not to make cop jokes or we're gonna push her in front of the bus." Jarel shrugged his shoulders, pretending to seem innocent.

Mrs. Rachel looked at the road and then back in her mirror. "Keep it up and Kelsey will have you unable to say the word *bus*. You know not to mess with her!"

The bus erupted with laughter, Brooke was bent over, crying with excitement. Kelsey smirked. Everyone knew how tough Kelsey was, her story.

After dominating on the court, Travis quietly slipped through the day. In class, his mind was still on last Sunday's conversation with Ms. Diane and Mr. Craig. Even at dinner that evening, he remained silent, thinking. The idea of being wanted and loved, made him feel special. His heart felt warm, safe in Garden County.

Ms. Diane and Mr. Craig knew, but they didn't push. He overheard the Moorings discussing later. "He needs time to process."

Travis needed time to think. But he also wanted to get the strain off his chest. After a couple of games before school, the next morning, Jarel and Travis grabbed breakfast in the cafeteria.

"Ms. Diane and Mr. Craig want me to stay with them..." Travis stated. "To adopt me, permanently." As if Jarel really needed the clarification. The two boys sat down, began to eat.

"That's awesome! Now I'll finally have someone cool enough to run with and that can ball!" He was so excited, he slapped Travis's arm a couple times. Almost enough to irk, but Travis was more caught up in the idea of staying in one place for a long time.

"It's not that simple."

"What do you mean? You wanna be here right? I know this isn't the coolest place to live. But Ms. Diane and Mr. Craig are good people."

Travis shook his head.

"Oh man, I forgot. You still out there doing that yard work? They want you to pave the dirt court?"

"No, man. No, no, and no... although I wouldn't object to getting it paved. Or even making a bigger, regulation court. Don't tell anyone about this, not yet."

"About wanting the court paved or them adopting you? I know they love that court." Jarel winked and grinned.

"Man."

"Okay, I know. You're my boy. I got your back." Jarel took another bite of his sausage biscuit, then reached up and exchanged fist bumps with Travis. "But I'm telling you, man. If you stay here, we're gonna tear it up in high school. Then go to a big college like Auburn or LSU."

"I just want to get through today."

Jarel sighed. "It makes sense to me. I can't think of a better place to be than with Ms. Diane and Mr. Craig."

Travis flashbacked to Smiley Court Apartments, overhearing an argument between Uncle Eddy and Mom: *Cheryl, think about it. Travis would do great in Atlanta with me. You see how well he gets along with people here. It wouldn't be any different in Atlanta. He'll have opportunities that you and I didn't get growing up here. He can get exposed to some great things!*

"*Brrring! Brrring!*" The bell snapped him from the dingy apartments to Raymond Blake Middle School.

Maybe if I just get into a little bit of trouble or something, Ms. Diane and Mr. Craig will change their mind about wanting to adopt me. He went to throw away his trash.

"Don't even think about it," Dean Matts said. Travis froze. "You guys haven't said anything about playing in summer league. You're not going by me again without saying something."

"Well, Travis and I decided that we want 51% ownership in the team, naming, and exclusive rights. Plus we want shoe deals," Jarel declared.

"I hope you play better than you tell jokes," Dean Matts said.

"I'm getting a new physical. You know my folks are on top of that stuff." Jarel fist bumped with the dean-turned-mentor.

"Travis, are you gonna stick around this summer to see how we do basketball here? It gets pretty intense."

"We'll see." Travis adjusted his backpack. "I gotta figure out some stuff first."

"Mhm… y'all get to class before I get another email from your teachers. Especially you, Presell."

"Come on, man. You know some of those teachers are always tripping!" The boys walked out of the cafeteria and headed down the hall.

Trouble found Travis, again. This time, before school. Jarel and Travis dominated George's team in the first game, 11-4. But after George warned Jarel that he wouldn't take another loss.

This was familiar territory for Travis; he saw the same behavior when watching his uncle on the court at their apartment complex. Long-tenured residents knew Uncle Eddy could play ball. The newest residents always learned the hard way; watching Uncle Eddy serve an array of beautiful moves and jump shots, always failing to stop him. Then Eddy would turn around and lock the newbie down on the defensive end. "White Chocolate" was one popular nickname Uncle Eddy had in the neighborhood.

Jarel made a beautiful one-hand pass on the wing to Travis. He caught the ball in rhythm, turned and dribbled to the rim. He then exploded off two feet with his left hand guiding the ball. *Here comes George… I'm going over him… he won't go for the blo-*

As Travis released the ball, George released another forearm into Travis' gut. Travis flopped to the ground hard, like a wet rag.

"Umph!" Travis winced.

"Jeez, man," Jarel yelled as he jogged over to help his wingman back onto his feet.

George stood over Travis. His intimidating 6'5" frame. "No easy lay-ups." He turned around, walked off. Then yelled at his teammate.

"I'm good," Travis said as Jarel helped him up. "Let's win this."

The next play, Jaden passed to Jarel on the wing. He took a jab step and his defender stumbled back. He smiled, and then launched a high-arching twenty-foot jumper.

Swish! Nothing but net.

The next play, Jaden got open for a mid-range jumper. Travis maneuvered to the other side of the lane. He beat George the Giant to the spot. As he began to jump for the rebound, he felt someone pull him back on his left shoulder.

George bumped just enough to keep Travis's fingertips from touching the ball. But he didn't miss another crash-landing on the court.

"Yo, you need to chill out!" Jarel jogged over. This time he approached the giant, head-to-shoulder. Jaden and some others separated the two, while Travis staggered to his feet.

Man, its nice having someone that has your back. He refocused on the game. *3-0. Get to 7-0 and the game is over.*

George was persistent, though. After another long shot, he boxed Travis from getting the rebound, and attempted to hook him.

Gotcha. As he back-stepped behind George, he kicked out the big man's foot, causing him to topple to the ground like the Giant in *Jack and the Beanstalk.*

George jumped up and began shoving Travis, who pulled back his elbow and landed a punch square on the giant's jaw.

Dean Matts rushed to the hardtop and separated the boys. Another fight. Another consequence. For Travis, another suspension- this one for the next three days of school. Within an hour, Mr. Craig came to pick Travis up from school.

"You're going to work with me for the rest of the week. No hanging out at the house," he said. They climbed into his truck.

I can't believe I was stupid enough to get dragged into hitting George. They definitely aren't gonna keep me now.

He dropped his shoulders as the truck rolled into a parking lot. A small plaque by the glass doors greeted him. *Public Works Department.* Faded bricks, old trucks, and dead grass discouraged visitors.

"You got help today, boss?" A guy yelled as the two walked into the office.

"Yes, for the rest of the week," Mr. Craig looked over.

"Good, share the wealth. I got some drains I have to get my guys down in today. I could use the help!" The man shouted back as they walked into the building.

"Miss Elliott," Mr. Craig greeted. The two entered an open office area. "This is Travis, I told you about."

"Oh, hello," she greeted. A short lady wearing blue-framed glasses and a large smile looked up from her monitor. She wore bright, red lipstick and a black jacket. The small office wing was dimly lit and very cold. File cabinets lined two of the walls.

"He got suspended today. He'll be around for a couple days. Have him do some paperwork for you." He turned back to look at Travis. "If it's done wrong, we'll be here late fixing it." He walked into his office, picked up a bag, and then back outside towards the parking lot. "Call me if he finishes early or you're not sure what else he can do." He was gone.

"Oh! Hmm," Miss Elliott began. She walked from her desk to a stack of freshly printed papers. "Looks like you're going to be the paper boy today." She smiled broadly.

Travis spent his day organizing papers into stacks by colors. Then enveloping and placing them in mailboxes, delivering packages in the building, and helping clean the offices.

He hoped for downtime to go on a computer and check out highlights of last night's NBA games but that wasn't going to happen. Plus, Miss Elliott checked on him hourly, constantly watching, then typing on her phone. She received text messages for updates from Mr. Craig.

Mr. Craig pulled up around 1:00 pm with lunch. "Here's two sandwiches and water." He pulled a water bottle from the office refrigerator.

"That's it? You have some burgers and fries. And I get ham and cheese sandwiches?"

"Keep your hands to yourself, keep your butt in class and you can get something else." He walked off, passing out some sandwiches to a couple of people in the office. Travis slumped in a squeaky chair and munched. His day ended breaking down boxes out back.

On Thursday and Friday, Mr. Craig was ready to put Travis to work. So was the rest of the office. He hardly had any time to take a break, let alone eat his sandwich. He spent the first half of the day at Mr. Craig's office with more filing, sorting and stacking. The afternoon consisted of delivering mail and packages throughout the office building and more copying for Miss Elliott.

This is the last time I'm getting suspended from school, especially if I stay with them.

For dinner, Mr. Craig stopped at a local pizza shop. Travis got to pick the toppings on one of the pizzas. He chose pepperoni and pineapple.

"That's the last time I'm getting suspended," he declared. "I promise! The last three days were miserable." Mr. Craig smiled. They turned onto the dirt driveway and talked about basketball, while they hustled inside to set the table. Ms. Diane greeted her boys and continued preparing a salad. Within minutes, they were all seated in the dining room.

"I, uh, I have something to say," he said at the table. Ms. Diane, Mr. Craig and Jon quieted and looked at Travis. He fumbled with a folded piece of paper that he pulled out of his pocket and began.

Chapter 13

Travis's mind wandered in different directions while he reached into his pocket. He looked up at Ms. Diane, who had a huge smile on her face. Travis cleared his throat as he starred at the unfolded paper. Nervous was an understatement. Sweat beads popped on his forehead. Hands vibrated.

The paper shook while he tried to relax.

I can't do this. What was I thinking? He gazed around the room before settling back on the paper. Then took a quick sip. His hands shook, nearly spilling the fruit juice.

For the first time, Mr. Craig didn't seem intimidating.

Travis froze. He couldn't bring himself to say a word. He couldn't find the strength from within to say what he'd written down: about how much he grew to love Ms. Diane, how she became the kind of mother he never had. How she showed him more love in a few months than his biological mother did, how she seemed to get him, and knew what he needed before he could vocalize it.

His mouth moved. Nothing came out. He felt pitiful. Surely Jon would make fun of him on the bus Monday. The Moorings would have a great laugh at his expense, privately. They wouldn't take this moment seriously, no matter how much they tried.

Nonetheless, he made a valiant effort to continue.

Travis's volume remained on mute, like the television in the distance, unable to tell Mr. Craig what he wrote. Relying on speech and actions, he taught Travis a multitude of lessons without ever having to raise a hand. He knew how to correct, chastise and challenge him to be a better person. Mr. Craig impacted his life. Travis was learning how to make better decisions as a young man.

There were unwritten words on the paper about Jon. Travis had become a pest to Jon: all of the questions about adoption, adjusting to life in Easton, and living with the Moorings. Travis knew he'd been particularly difficult to be around when he first moved in. But Jon tolerated his misbehavior, offered advice and encouragement. He wanted Jon to know how much he appreciated it.

He cleared his throat for what felt like the hundredth time. It was time to open up. To be vulnerable. But growing up in foster care, this was forbidden.

"I just want to apologize for all the stupid stuff I did, getting in trouble on the bus, at school. I won't do it again. Love y'all."

He slumped into his chair, unable to look up. The words he uttered were the opposite of the notes he'd scribbled onto the paper. He failed, again. Unable to open up with the closest people in his life, with himself.

But before he could take a second deep breath, he felt arms wrapped around him. First, Ms. Diane came around the table. Travis felt her tears drop onto his head. Then a hairy arm brushed Travis's face. When he thought he couldn't bear any more weight, a heavier mass laid atop the three.

He was wrapped with love. Like the rap song he heard, *Good Hands*. He finally felt like he no longer had to control every situation or conversation involving him. He could surrender the need for power. Someone wanted to help him, love him.

"That was so sweet, hun!" She held him tight. Her embrace whispered, "*I know what you wanted to say. I love you.*"

"We love you, Travis." Mr. Craig's body crackled as he stood up. Ms. Diane maintained her grip. "You, Jon, Neal, Sherman, and Tyreese. You each make our hearts grow."

Who?

Mr. Craig continued before Travis asked. "Now, let's clean up so Diane and I can deliver a beating to you guys out back."

Shooting some hoops. Sounds like the perfect end to a long week. He rushed to the back porch and pulled out an old pair of New Balances. Black with grey stitching. The same faded kicks he wore the evening he moved in. Those were now his outdoor shoes.

The Moorings and Jon followed outside. Just as they began taking shots on the court, raindrops started to fall.

"Aww, no basketball tonight!" Ms. Diane said.

"It's just rain," Travis pleaded. "C'mon, weren't you the same gal that bragged about loving the sound of chains more than the pop of the net?"

"Yes! But I never liked shooting in the mud. It takes away my handles!" she answered.

"So you don't do the mud court anymore?"

"No sir. Maybe it's time we look into paving the court." She turned to Mr. Craig, smiling.

"Maybe so," he agreed.

One thing was sure — it was time for change. Everyone knew, and everyone was ready.

"What's up?" Jarel greeted. Travis walked toward his assigned seat on the bus.

"Hey, man," Travis said. He sat by his best friend and wingman.

"So?" Jarel began.

"So… what?" clueless about Jarel's inquiry.

"C'mon man, summer league!"

"Dude, I don't know. We gotta see. I'm not sure how long I'll be here." He thought about their last conversation. His life was shifting from a lane of constant change to declaring a permanent home.

"Man, stop acting like you don't want to stick around. At least stay for the summer!" Jarel pleaded. "See how good we can be before you move."

Travis sat still. Emotions flew all over, like fireworks. The excitement of playing organized basketball for the first time, having adults in his life who really cared for him. But insecurity of how the next steps, and fear if the adoption wasn't approved, pulled him back down.

"What happened with that thing Ms. Diane said to you?" Jarel dug for more information.

"Dude, we're not gonna talk about that right now."

"Bruh, for real." Jarel pleaded, turning to face his favorite pick-up basketball teammate.

Travis was desperate to change the topic. "Are we balling today?"

"Yes." Jarel shook his head, frowned. Playing ball before school was a no-brainer. "Bring your *A* game today without trying to fight! Wait, you're allowed to play?"

"Ah, shoot. I forgot. Dean Matts said I can't go there for a week."

"No sweat, man. I'll hold it down for you." The boys fist-bumped. "What are you gonna do instead?"

"Dude, I don't even know." But he had an idea. Find Brooke, keep trying to get on her good side, hope Kelsey wouldn't be there. "Maybe go to the library and do some make-up work."

He checked with Dean Matts once he got off the bus, to see if any teachers left classwork for him during his suspension.

"You can check with your teachers *except* Mrs. Ranson. Understand?" Dean Matts said firmly.

"Yes sir!" Travis saluted.

"If she says something, you're on your own." He ignored Travis' silliness, turned back to the bus loop, then radioed that a seventh grader was going through the building with permission.

After he gathered the packets of work, Travis headed to the library. He planned to get a head start on the mounds of homework that would swallow him after school. Settled at a dark walnut, rectangular table near the bookshelves and opened his bag. The first assignment was for the U.S. History class. It contained two articles about the same event – Civil Rights events in the South. While reading, he reflected on the trip to Atlanta.

One packet down, four to go.

"Ah, he knows how to pull objects out of a backpack!"

He jumped, looked around for the mystery voice.

"Easy, tiger," Brooke joked. She walked around a small bookshelf and sat at the table, across from Travis. "What are you working on?"

"Hey. Just trying to catch up on work from last week." Travis felt the temperature rise in the library. He tried to balance between sounding excited and annoyed. He paused. "Do you want to take a look at it? Math isn't really my strongest subject."

"Oh, no!" She leaned back. "I hate math. But I can do science. Ironic, huh?"

"Hmm. Well, maybe we can look at it together? Jon says you learn from teaching."

The librarian peeked around the corner. "You guys need to keep it down or get out." Typical old lady with glasses. Brown cardigan.

Brooke and Travis nodded their heads in compliance, ushering silent *Yes ma'ams*. She turned back. He stared. She seemed much different than the first time he gazed into her hazel eyes. Now there was life, energy, a tad bit of joy, he felt. He wondered how someone who went through so much had any joy at all.

"Tell me about yourself," she countered, quietly.

Travis, caught off-guard, felt his palms getting sticky, sweaty. His eyes bulged.

"I know a little bit about you. But I kinda want to know more, before rumors about you get out. You know, small town. Stories change, like the fish that was about *this* big." Her hands moved farther apart, a smile grew on her face. "You do some dumb stuff, like all the other boys. I wanna know if that's really you. What's your story?"

"*Life is all about decisions, man,*" he recalled Uncle Eddy saying. "*You gotta know when to take the shot, and when to pass. But here's the thing- sometimes when you think its best to shoot, you should really pass. And other times when you think you should pass, you're supposed to take the shot.*" This never made sense. But the older Travis got, the more basketball he played, the more he recognized decisions must be made, and what Uncle Eddy meant.

Take the shot. This may be the path to really earn her trust. And when else will I get to talk without the man-hater around?

Fifteen minutes seemed like seconds. In a hushed tone, he shared stories about being a foster kid. Quick stops in Hoover and suburban Birmingham and remembered some of his brief stay in Florence. He didn't say much about his mother or Uncle Eddy. Brooke asked questions, but not about his parents. Nor did she offer any information about herself. He felt like the unfolded piece of paper he had the previous Friday night. Vulnerable, exposed.

"What about you?" He tried to change the topic.

Brooke posed an inquisitive glare. "Well, I like pink PB teen backpacks!" She grinned, stood up, pushed in her chair and winked at Travis.

"What?! Come on, now!" He quickly lowered his voice before the old librarian would appear.

"*Brrring! Brrring!*"

"Time for class!" Brooke smiled and walked out of the library, headed towards the seventh grade wing.

Man, I said all that. I bet she's gonna use that information against me. Wrong. He couldn't have been further from the truth.

Chapter 14

"It's the B-boy!" Kelsey shouted.

Travis moped onto the bus, exhausted, and in no mood for Kelsey's nonsense. He'd been up late the previous night completing assignments. Still sour how their conversation ended the previous morning, he saw Brooke sitting by her cousin in Seat 14.

Brooke knew how Travis felt, but gave him a quick smile anyway.

"*B*-boy? His name starts with a '*T*'." Jarel and Travis exchanged fist bumps. "I know you're not a big fan of learning the alphabet!"

"He's the *B*-boy because your knucklehead friend can't handle things that start with the letter B." Kelsey restrained herself from popping Jarel.

"And you can't handle anything that starts with one of the 26 letters!" Jarel clowned. Other kids laughed, but quieted down as Kelsey cracked her knuckles.

"Don't make me jump on you!" she warned. "Your buddy doesn't do well with the bus, backpacks, or basketball. Do you need me to spell it out?"

Jarel glanced around. "Since we're talking about the letter B, I know *one* thing he's into." He nodded his head at Brooke and turned away.

"What's that mean?" Kelsey asked.

"You'll figure it out when you learn the alphabet."

Travis shook his head and leaned against the window. *Play it cool. No one will notice.*

Travis headed straight to the library when the bus arrived at school. He wrestled in his backpack, reaching for homework packets. Then grimaced about the assignments not finished.

"That'll be the last time you get suspended, huh?" chirped a familiar voice.

Travis turned his shoulder just enough to catch a glimpse of her curls. He turned forward to face the table, steaming.

"Look, I'm really sorry about yesterday. I'll talk today if you want." Brooke slid into the chair across from him. "Maybe I'll even help you with that Social Studies assignment."

"I know my history," he snapped. "I mean… Ms. Diane and I studied already. Anyway, I did that work already." Beads of sweat rolled down his temple.

"Really?" Brooke leaned back. "Up for a little quiz, buddy?"

Buddy? Maybe I am making progress with her.

"Three branches of our government. What are they?"

"Easy. Legislative, Judicial…" He paused. Sweat dripped. "And… Executive. Yes!"

"Difference between longitude and latitude?" She smirked.

"One measures location horizontally and the other measures location vertically." He smiled back.

"Which is which? That's part of the question, Einstein."

"Latitude measures up and down, and longitude goes sideways."

"Missed shot. One for two," she grinned. "Next question. True or false; Alabama was one of the thirteen colonies."

"False. Georgia was the southern-most colony." His voice rose with restored confidence.

"Whisper. Anyways, that was easy." She smiled. "Another true or false question. The 13th amendment gave blacks the right to vote."

Too easy. The thirteenth amendment ended slavery, the Emancipation Proclamation. But did it say anything about the right to vote?

"False!" His whisper was a soft shriek.

Brooke frowned.

"Got the put-back dunk!" Travis imitated a Shaquille O'Neal-styled, two-hand dunk.

Her eyes changed from a frown to an evil smile. "When did the United States officially become a free country?"

"I know you want me to say July 4th, 1776… but that's too easy. The Americans had to *earn* their freedom. The correct answer is the year 1783. That's when England recognized the United States as an independent country!" Travis did his best James Harden impression, pretending to hold a huge pot and stir like a chef.

"Three out of five." Brooke commented. "I believe that'd be a 60%... which is a *D*."

"*D* is passing, right?" he smiled.

"Yup, but I believe the girls on the team say '*Cs get degrees.*' Tell me about Atlanta. And don't say you came just to watch our game, because you only came to one out of four!" She fidgeted in her seat. Rested her head in hands, elbows on the table.

Travis complied. He was thrilled that she wanted to hear about his spring break trip.

"*Brrring! Brrring!*"

"Same time and place tomorrow?"

"Maybe." Brooke smiled as she grabbed her backpack. "Or maybe you should get some work done. You look like you need a nap." And she was gone, with her curly black hair trailing her as she skipped out of the library.

"What are you doing up here?" Brooke ran into Travis while waiting in the front office. She sat in a chair by a closed door, with blinds shut. He rested in the chair next to her, leaning forward. Backpack still on, his head facing her red and black team softball shoes.

"Looking for Dean Matts. I didn't see him at the bus loop. I figured he could help me brush up on some of those Social Studies questions. What about you?"

"I was looking to see if Ms. Hope was going to be in today."

"Who's that?"

"The school counselor. She's here two days per week, and at the high school the rest of the time. Come on, let's get out of here." She nudged Travis.

"Everything cool?"

"No," she said. Travis stopped, as if he was going to swoop in like Superman to save her from danger. "Some jerk got the wrong shade of pink for my backpack," she giggled.

He couldn't tell if it was a real or fake laugh. They didn't talk much in the library. Brooke focused on a Social Studies project. She flipped between three books, placing sticky notes here and there. Travis stopped working and stared in awe.

"The answers to Math are not on my forehead," she stated.

"Oh, sorry. Why are you looking through those books and using sticky notes?"

"It helps me take notes, and get some ideas." She continued flipping pages, keeping her head down. Eventually she smiled and added, "Five for five, son."

"*Brrring! Brrring!*"

Travis smirked. "More like three for three this week. You must have some device in your head that says when the bell will ring."

"Ha-ha!" She packed up her books. "See ya on the bus."

The next day, Brooke finally walked with Travis from the bus. They navigated other students, heading to the library.

"Go ahead, young playa!" Jarel punched the air. "She better not keep you from playing ball next week!"

Kelsey glared at Travis and smacked her right fist into her left hand as a warning.

"I hope you're not threatening Travis or Jarel," a voice boomed.

Kelsey jumped. "Dean Matts, you know I'm too sweet to hurt anyone."

Jarel turned around and yelled. "That's a lie! The devil is alive!"

Travis helped Brooke with her Social Studies project. She ran ideas by him and he asked questions that she hadn't thought of.

"Maybe you can write about Reconstruction?" he suggested.

She'd shake her head, focus back on her paper, and then sigh aloud. After a couple deep breaths, she would ask a question. The process repeated itself.

"How the Emancipation Proclamation helped the North win the war? Pick a side for the Missouri-Kansas battle?"

Eventually, he recommended a topic that Brooke approved. "Write about Dred Scott. What would you say if you

were his lawyer?" He smiled. "We make a pretty good team!"
Then held his hand up for a high-five.

She looked up at his hand and immediately cowered, jumped back and ducked behind her books. Before Travis could make a joke, Brooke shoved her books in her backpack and rushed out of the library.

"Wait, what's wrong? What'd I say?" Travis quickly stood up. *What did I do?*

Travis rushed outside to the dirt court after school. He needed to clear his head with all the drama in his life. There were some things to look forward to if he stayed in Garden County: living with the Moorings, playing ball with Jarel, and figuring out Brooke.

Chling! He was on fire, making every shot possible. One-dribble jumpers, fancy ball-handling moves and layups at the rim, and shooting the deep ball.

He thought about Smiley Court Apartments – asking his mom for food and Cheryl saying *No*, while she guzzled the last sip of juice from the carton. About the times Uncle Eddy took him shopping at the used clothing store. The tragic night that changed his life.

Clank! Travis went from hot to cold. The ball bounced everywhere except in the rim.

Like an angel sent from above, Ms. Diane hollered from the porch. "Make your next shot so you can come wash up for dinner!" It was like the rim opened up on her demand. He looked at her, then the rim and launched a beautiful jump shot. *Nothing but rattling chains.*

"Ms. Diane." Travis jogged up the steps.

"Yes, hun."

His head tilted down toward her feet. She gently touched his chin and lifted until he looked into her eyes.

"You guys really want to adopt me?"

She smiled, "Yes. But it only works if you want to be here, too."

He rested his hands on his hips. Reminisced on past foster homes. Alan and Virginia's fancy, suburban home. Having to be so tidy. Then about the grouch, Mrs. Bermas and disdain. She didn't pay much attention to Travis, unless something broke. Although Kage, Kedrick, Kyron, or Korbin may have been responsible for the damage, they never got in trouble. He finally responded. "Okay. I kind of want to be here, too."

"Kind of?" she smiled.

Travis nodded his head, then walked into the house. He stopped down in hall and turned back to Ms. Diane. "No, not kind of. I *really* do want to be here."

Chapter 15

The next evening, Travis munched through dinner. The adoption process took up more and more of his mind. *Would Ms. Diane have said anything about adopting me if they didn't think I wanted to stay with them? What if I tell them I don't want to be adopted? Would they still keep trying?*

"Did you get to play basketball this week before school?" Ms. Diane asked.

"No ma'am." He replied in low, mopey tones. Then nibbled through small spoonfuls of cheese grits.

"Do you get to play next week?"

"Yes ma'am."

"What'd you do this week in the mornings?" Mr. Craig tried to spark life into dinner.

"Just school work." He debated the pros and cons of living with the Moorings. *It'd be nice to know I'm wanted. I have my own room. Ms. Diane and Mr. Craig are good people – they've done pretty good.*

He scanned the dining room. His eyes roamed looking for an escape. They landed on his picture hanging on the wall. One of the adults snagged a nice action shot of him shooting outside. Grey t-shirt, black shorts. The barn in the background. There were some photos of Jon and some other guys, none Travis recognized.

Could you beat this? Good food, nice place- basketball court right here, four-wheelers. The first thing Ms. Diane did was take me to buy clothes- that didn't happen at other places.

Jon is better than the other jerks I had to live with. He had spent more time asking Jon about the process of adopting. Going to court. Interviews with counselors. The steps.

What if me and Jarel end up hating each other? I'd be stuck with him for another five years of school.

"How's it going with Brooke?" Jon chipped in.

Travis's Kool-Aid rolled down the wrong pipe, causing him to cough. His eyes popped. Right leg shook rapidly. He stuttered.

"Come on, man," Jon said. "It's obvious that you like her. Maybe you were trying to make up for what you did, at first. But I hear that something more going on."

"It's cool. We just talk about sports and stuff." Travis sighed, reluctant to get words out.

"Mhm," Mr. Craig said. "Let's get this table cleared and figure out what movie to watch tonight."

Jon stood up, then took the boys' plates to the kitchen.

"College basketball season ended. Let's see if we have a basketball movie." Mr. Craig continued.

"How about *Space Jam*?" Ms. Diane recommended. Then took a sip of water.

"Come on." Jon hollered from the kitchen. Motioned for Travis to help, then added. "That's so kiddy."

"Kiddy but also a classic," Mr. Craig responded.

"Who doesn't like to watch MJ dominate?" Ms. Diane added.

"What about *Blue Chips*?" Jon asked.

"Travis, you got my back? Come on, now!" Ms. Diane stood and stretched, then crossed her arms while leaning against the door frame.

"Oh, uh," Travis stammered. He made two trips, taking cups, bowls and leftover food back to the kitchen. Even amidst the swirl of emotions in his head, he craved the evenings of playful jousting among the Moorings.

"Well?" Ms. Diane faced the unknown pictures on the wall, then turned around with a huge smile on her face.

"I've seen *Space Jam* before, but I've never seen *Blue Chips*," Travis said. He hated to disagree with her.

"Ugh, I should write a book about my problems!" She smacked her hands on the table. "Life as the only girl!"

He jumped. Lowered his head. He had disappointed her, again.

"Don't be fooled, Travis." Mr. Craig stood up, then walked to the living room. "She's being dramatic… Jon, looks like we are taking a loss today. I'll get the popcorn going."

"So what movie are we watching?" Travis was puzzled.

Jon turned on the television and scrolled through a list. "Neither of those are still on."

"*Coach Carter!*" Mr. Craig and Ms. Diane yelled, nearly in unison. Everyone settled into the living room. Mr. Craig reclined in his chair, Ms. Diane on her favorite spot on the couch, and Jon sprawled on the carpet. Travis strolled into the living room before stretching out on the couch.

The movie began with Ken Carter's alma mater, Richmond High, hosting a private school where Carter's son is on the team. For Richmond, the game displayed a collection of turnovers, terrible shots, even worse decision-making, and lack of team comradery.

The opponent gathered a collection of dunks, threes, and pretty passing. They looked like a professional team scrimmaging against kids.

"Looks like the Bad News Bears!" Jon laughed.

"They look like your team!" Mr. Craig blurted.

"*Ring, Ring! Ring, Ring!*" Ms. Diane's phone vibrated in the kitchen.

"Is that my phone?" She hurried to the counter. Eyebrows shriveled, lips tightened. "I thought I put it on *do not disturb*."

"Must be one of the boys." Mr. Craig sat up. His eyes followed Ms. Diane. "I hope they're okay."

One of the boys? What is he talking about? They have kids? Bewildered, Travis shrugged his shoulders.

"Oh, it's Neal!" Ms. Diane replied. Then turned her back to the television. "Hey baby, how are you?"

Who is Neal?

Mr. Craig clicked play, then lowered the volume. The movie continued.

"Oh yeah? That's good… Really? Coming here? No, that's great! Of course we have room! Yes… tomorrow? Okay. What time? Okay… yup! Yes, you can meet him. Jon is doing well."

Travis struggled to eavesdrop on the conversation. He shifted on the couch to hear. But Ms. Diane went from the dining room to the porch to talk. He saw her sit in a rocking chair.

How does this Neal character know about me? Could that be the adoption agency worker? No, that was one of her kids… but maybe he did work for the agency.

Ms. Diane rejoined the group before the movie ended. When she sat on the couch, she made an announcement. Her eyes beamed with joy. "Neal will be in town this weekend! He's flying into Tuscaloosa tomorrow afternoon."

"That's great!" Jon sat up. "How long will he be here?"

"For the weekend. He has class Monday," said Ms. Diane.

The family seemed oblivious to his bewilderment. He scratched his head. Tilting it sideways, he hoped they would catch on.

"Look at the wall." Jon pointed to the collection of pictures in the dining room. The same photos Travis noticed during dinner. There were pictures of five young boys, all action shots. One playing football. The other two in basketball games. There was a picture of Jon lifting weights, *squatting*, he'd corrected the new kid. Lastly, Travis's basketball picture he recognized.

"Neal is the one in the middle," said Ms. Diane. "He was the third one we adopted."

Third one? Travis had seen the photos hanging before, but never considered the other faces next to his and Jon's.

Ms. Diane turned her body towards Travis and narrated the story; how the Moorings began as foster parents, then adopted other boys, long before Travis was even born.

Travis learned when Jon first came into the Mooring's home, Neal was a senior at Garden County High School. He'd lived with Ms. Diane and Mr. Craig for five years. Originally from Mobile, he had bounced around during elementary and middle school. Now he's a sophomore wide receiver on Mount Union College's football team, a small Division III school in eastern Ohio. They won a National Championship team his freshmen year. Back in high school, he was known as the Ed McCaffrey of high school football.

When Neal moved in, the Moorings raised Sherman. He now lived in Memphis. Sherman was fascinated by Ms. Diane's gentleness, consistent no matter how much trouble he caused. His behavior improved, now in his last semester of college, preparing to go into law enforcement soon. He had nearly squandered a track scholarship but academic probation helped him refocus.

Before Sherman, Tyreese lived with the Moorings. He was the first college graduate of the boys. He ended up here because of his parents' incarceration. While playing college basketball at Louisiana Tech, he frequently came home to counsel and spend time with Sherman. The experience of mentoring, led him to become a high school science teacher and basketball coach in St. Louis.

Now it makes sense. No wonder Ms. Diane always knew what to do or say. And how she could predict when I was gonna do something stupid. She had plenty of experience before I got here. All these months of living here, and I never thought to ask.

Chapter 16

The next week Travis's mind sputtered. He learned that the adoption process was challenging. Adoption meetings and court hearings lay ahead. Plus, state tests were approaching at school. He worried like the rest of his peers. It was late in the school year when he began taking school serious. *Too little, too late*, he feared.

On top of the adoption, school, and basketball, Travis wondered how things would go with Brooke. *Was she only being nice because she thought I would move soon?*

He quickly found his version of therapy. A couple of mornings of basketball before school helped Travis calm down. Playing with Jarel was fun, because it almost always resulted in a win. The morning lulled.

Dean Matts plopped onto a seat at the boys table as lunch began. "What's up?"

"I'm trying to get him to work on stuff for basketball." Jarel sighed, nodded his head towards Travis.

"Hey, if he doesn't want to play, you can't make him." He scanned the cafeteria, seemed to be looking out for more chaos.

"It's not that," Travis defended. "I don't know if I'll even be here!" His anger rose, upset over his hopeless situation. He couldn't control the outcome. And Jarel pestering Travis about playing summer league basketball didn't help. It only added fuel to the fire of home, school, basketball… life.

"Breathe, youngster," Uncle Eddy would say when I got worked up.

"Breathe, Travis," Dean Matts said. "I get it. Take care of what you can control, and let everything else be."

That afternoon rain ruined a much-needed time of refuge on the dirt court. "Man! I can't shoot today!" Travis stormed into the house.

"Oh, no," Ms. Diane agreed. "You don't want to get all muddy. I understand."

But he needed an escape. A break. "Just promise, if the adoption papers go through, we will get the court redone," he pleaded. "If not concrete or asphalt, something."

"You got it, hun." She smiled.

His downhill spiral continued for the remainder of the week. He thought getting kicked out of class for letting a student borrow a pencil was bad – but today struck a new low. He rushed into Mrs. Ranson's class, afraid he'd be late.

Yes! He slid into his desk, leaned back and took a deep breath.

"Barely made it!" Brooke commented. She reached over and gave him an extra firm pat on the arm.

"Ah, yup! Just my luck!" He laughed. He was glad for new assigned seats. His desk was now next to Brooke. She frowned.

"Excuse me," Mrs. Ranson yelled.

Travis jumped.

"We don't talk like that here!" She marched over to the front of Travis's row. Then crossed her arms. Her foot tapped on the floor.

What's she talking about?

"We are not swearing in this classroom." Her eyes glared. "Get your stuff and get out!" One hand on her hip. The other pointed towards the door.

"But, I didn't say anyth…" he pleaded.

"Get out!" she shouted. "And go straight to the dean's office!"

Everyone turned and watched as Travis dragged his feet from his seat. He slowly moved from the back row, out of the classroom, and down the hall. Then paused outside Dean Matts's office, his head bowed.

The door opened so fast, it nearly knocked Travis off balance. Dean Matts rushed out with a large white Styrofoam cup in his hand. "Oops!" he yelped. He turned around. "You okay?"

"Yes…" Travis kept his head down.

"What happened?" He glanced at his watch. "Were you in Mrs. Ranson's class?"

"Yes, sir." Travis sounded like a sad puppy.

"Come on." Dean Matts headed back to his desk and sat down. "What happened? And, the truth, please. She'll be emailing or calling me shortly."

"She thinks I cursed. But all I said is "just my *luck*." I came in before the bell rang and rushed to my seat. Brooke said something funny about barely being on time." Travis's hands flailed. "And I said *just… my… luck…* " He spoke slowly. And clearly.

Dean Matts rubbed his scruffy beard. Then leaned back in his office chair and rocked. After a few seconds he interlocked his fingers and rested his hands in his lap.

Travis leaned forward. "I promise I didn't say anything else! I, I don't know what else to say! I didn't curse! You see how much I've been trying to stay out of trouble." He paused. "You know how difficult she is. She's always causing problems with students. Remember that time she sent me here for letting another kid borrow a pencil?"

"Hmm." Dean Matts spun from side to side in his chair. "Just do your work here for the period. I'll see what she says, and we'll deal with it later. For now, no referral."

Yes! Whew! Travis went from sad and depressed to ecstatic and relieved. This was the first break he'd caught all week.

His day got better when Brooke came by the bus loop. She hung out with Jarel and Travis while they waited for their bus. She plopped between the two boys as they waited on a concrete bench, catching them off guard.

"What's up guys?" Brooke playfully elbowed the duo.

"Ah!" Jarel jumped.

"Oh, please. Don't be so soft! You're acting like Kyrie Irving. Do you have a busted kneecap too?"

"I will if we keep hanging out with you!" Jarel said as he rubbed his left thigh.

"Oh, come on! Don't be such a baby. You're gonna let a *girl* hurt you?" Brooke laughed, turning her head between them.

Travis's face got serious, fearful, when Brooke looked at him. *Kelsey.* His mind flashbacked the powerful, unexpected swing and force of the punch she delivered. He was confident everyone on the bus could hear the *smack* of her first connecting with his cheek.

Brooke dropped her head, quickly changing the subject. "What are you guys doing this afternoon?"

"Shooting hoops, balling on Travis!" Jarel held his right hand as if he was frozen after making a jump shot.

"Oh, man! Travis, you're gonna take it like that?" she laughed.

"I'm going to just let him talk now. Tomorrow morning he'll be the quiet one on the bus," Travis said, then jumped. "Brooke! You heard what I said in class, right? I didn't swear."

She rolled her eyes. "I know you didn't. Mrs. Ranson is just annoying. Every school has that one teacher all the kids hate. By the way, you used that expression '*just my luck*' wrong. You're supposed to say it when something *bad* happens."

"Come on, man. I'll teach you about school and Brooke will teach you English." Jared shook his head in agreement. "Then tomorrow, Mrs. Ranson can try to teach you math!"

"Hah! Where are y'all playing? At your place?" Brooke faced Travis.

"Yup." He had never referred to the Moorings' home as *his* house, *his* home, *his* place. It had a really nice ring. This was the first time he had thought of a place as home other than Smiley Court Apartments in Montgomery.

After six games on the dirt court, both boys were covered in sweat, with three wins each. Neither was ready to give in, as Travis fought back to win the last game 11-8.

"Home court advantage is about to be eliminated." Jarel checked the ball with Travis. "I *almost* feel bad for this win I'm about to get."

Saying nothing, Travis pounded the ball onto the dirt, then backed down Jarel to the post. Jarel tried to reach around to steal the ball but Travis spun to the opposite side and lofted a gentle left-handed shot.

The chains rattled. *1-0.*

With a warrior spirit, Jarel scored four straight points with an array of one dribble pull-ups went straight through the rim.

Travis responded with a strong lay-up as Jarel tried to slap his arms. *And one!* He smiled. The next shot for Travis was a twenty-foot jumper. 4-3, Jarel.

The two players went point-for-point for the next handful of possessions.

"10-9." Jarel checked the ball with Travis.

"Nothing easy." Travis crept up to guard Jarel closely. *Nowhere for him to go.* He swiped for the ball.

Jarel stepped forward, squeezing the ball with both hands. This forced Travis to hop a half-step backwards. As he slid back, Jarel dribbled around him, going straight to the rim.

Travis tried to recover, but he was too late. Jarel leaned towards the basket and tossed up a gentle floater. It banged off the backboard and fizzled through the chain nets.

11-9.

"Don't worry. We'll run it back soon." Jarel reached out to give Travis a fist bump. "Good game. Let's clean up so you can do my math work. Mrs. Ranson is killing me."

She was killing everyone, and would continue her onslaught towards Travis on Friday.

"Hey, can I borrow a pencil?" Travis mouthed to Brooke.

She smiled, reached in her backpack and handed him her pink mechanical pencil. Travis frowned, but reluctantly took it.

"Well?" Mrs. Ranson asked. "Not coming to class prepared, now? I guess using foul language wasn't enough!"

Travis didn't respond. This was a no-win situation with Mrs. Ranson.

"So not only are we unprepared, but we are going to sit there and be defiant and ignore the teacher?" She reached over to her desk and began writing on a yellow sheet of paper. "Well maybe Dean Matts will have a pencil in ISD that you can borrow."

I guess there is a negative to staying in Easton. He took the pass and strolled to the dean's office. *At least I get a break from her.*

But soon there would be a tougher lady waiting to challenge Travis.

"Hello, I'm..."

"Oh my goodness," Ms. Diane hollered. She opened the front door wide, and stepped onto the porch. "I can't believe it. Girl, you haven't changed a bit. Not since we played!"

The lady at the door rested her hands on her hip, with a steely gaze.

"Oh man! That was so long ago, but it almost feels like yesterday!" Ms. Diane grinned.

"Yes, a long time ago. Can we get down to business?" The lady progressed. "I'm Megan Brandock, with Alabama Department of Human Resources. I'm here to interview you and Travis." She smiled. "Shouldn't this be fun?"

"Ah," Ms. Diane crossed her arms, only for a second. She pointed her finger at the guest. Her tone sounded firm. "A title and a fancy business card are no match. Come in."

For the next hour and a half, Ms. Diane and Travis were grilled with questions.

"What do you do for a living? How long have you lived at this address? What is your income history like? Have you ever been arrested? How long have you been fostering children? What does your spouse do for work? Have you ever intentionally neglected to share information with your foster child's case worker? What has been the worst incident or injury a child has ever had in your care?"

Travis stood around the corner from the dining room, intently listening to the questions. The last one asked to Ms. Diane sent shivers up his spine. The incident when he ran into the woods was probably the worst event that happened while the Moorings raised other people's children. It had to have been. Travis was sure of it.

Contrary to Ms. Diane, he slouched in his seat, stumbling through his answers. He had been through interviews before, but this one was different. The "right" answer was needed to make the adoption a success.

"What do you like most about the foster parents? What chores do they make you do? Do you feel safe here? How do you like school? Have they made you do anything that you don't believe is okay? Where have you gone for trips? Do you get along with other children in the home? Does your host feed you three times a day? Clothing? Have you gotten hurt or needed to go to the doctor while you lived with this host family?"

Another slam dunk for the unfriendly, old lady.

Did Ms. Diane tell her about the incident in the woods? he wondered. *She's an honest person, I'm sure she did. And, if I lie, this lady is going to think that Ms. Diane is trying to trick me into lying to cover up.*

"The snake bite was bad. I had to stay in the hospital for a couple days." Travis gave another bad answer. Disappointed, he shook his head.

The lady closed her binder, and smirked. She straightened up. Thick, gray-rimmed glasses seemed to frown. Then stood up and shouted a disheartening farewell. She told them they would be in contact shortly. Her body language was cold. Not even facing the sweet, wonderful Ms. Diane for the last words. "Good luck."

"Who was that lady?" Travis asked after Ms. Diane closed the door.

"The adoption agency lady," she answered. "Didn't I tell you they were coming today?"

"Yes, but you acted like you knew her. I heard when you answered the door."

"Yeah," Ms. Diane smirked. Then let loose a deep belly laugh. "That old battle ax? That's Megan Brandock. We played volleyball against each other in high school."

"Really? What's so funny about that?"

"Well, she played for Dixie High School. We beat them my junior *and* senior year for the state championship."

"Oh. Sounds like there's some bad blood."

"Well, it only gets worse."

"Oh, no. Don't tell me she had a crush on Mr. Craig!"

"She will once she meets him. I also beat her cousin in the girls' basketball championship game my senior year."

"Talk about bad blood!" Travis said. "Are we gonna be able to pull this one out?"

"Honey, one thing about me, I don't lose."

From what he heard, winning was all Ms. Diane did on the court. But this was a different ball game. Travis would soon learn about 'the game within the game'.

Chapter 17

"Y'all come over for lunch!" Ms. Diane said. It sounded more like a demand than invitation. Sunday church service ended. A dozen people were still socializing in the auditorium or outside soaking in the beautiful, warm sunshine.

"Are you sure?" Ms. Bridgette looked around.

"Yes, I insist. We have plenty of food and room at the table," said Ms. Diane.

"Well, I don't see why not. I guess it worked out perfectly because I didn't cook last night," Ms. Bridgette said.

Different emotions swept through Travis as he overheard the ladies talk. The best example for a basketball junkie is the feeling a player has when they're playing in the NBA Finals. Part excitement about the upcoming opportunity to win a championship, something that they've worked hard for, and have always wanted. But also nervous, even frightful. A chance that everything could go wrong; and no matter how much they try, things (or the game) keep getting worse.

The last time Brooke and Kelsey were at the Moorings' house was after Travis threw Brooke's backpack out the bus window. The same night he disappeared into the woods.

"Travis, can you show the girls how to set up the table? Cups, plates and silverware?" Ms. Diane asked while she began delegating a long list of tasks. "Jon, start getting the drinks ready," she continued. "Bridgette, can you come help me get the food ready? Craig, can you adjust the thermostat? It's gonna be a little warm in here, especially in the kitchen. And make sure the living room looks nice."

Everyone marched, completing the various missions as assigned.

Travis was probably the most excited of the group. His nerves finally lowered as he began showing the girls where the forks and spoons and napkins were.

"Do you know what she made?" Kelsey asked as the three moved around the table.

"No. Maybe chicken and mac and cheese," Travis answered. "Whatever it is, I'm sure it'll be good. It beats what I had before moving here."

"That's the truth. She can cook!" Brooke added. "We came over for New Years. She made some black-eyed peas and something else. It was delicious." She smiled. The dining room seemed brighter than ever. Like a special light shined when Brooke spoke.

"Travis, can you cook?" Kelsey challenged.

"Of course I can," he grinned. "I make the meanest grilled cheese sandwich ever. What else do you think I ate all these years?" Travis reminisced back to the hapless days with Ms. Bermas. Late-nights in the kitchen, hunting for food so the older boys wouldn't grab whatever meal he could muster.

"Man, that's not cooking," Kelsey said.

"What about pasta?" asked Travis.

"Cooking noodles?" Kelsey sucked her teeth. "Typical, helpless *boy*."

"I don't remember the last time you cooked anything," Brooke came to Travis's defense. He spun his head around quickly, caught off guard that she countered her cousin's meanness.

"Me either!" Ms. Bridgette barged in holding a steaming pot by the handles. "Set the mat over there. You sure are demanding for someone that doesn't even make Kool-Aid!"

Brooke and Travis laughed as Jon joined them at the table.

Mr. Craig followed behind. "Are y'all ready to eat?"

"Just about," Ms. Diane hollered from the kitchen. "I need someone to bring a tray over here. Today!"

Travis and Brooke responded to her orders. He pulled a rectangular tray from a lower cabinet.

"This is the cornbread. You be careful with that. You know how Craig is about his cornbread… "You gone eat your cornbread?"" She laughed at her impression from an old movie.

"I know Mr. Craig will eat it all!" Brooke laughed.

"Haha! Be gentle with that pot of vegetables," Ms. Diane instructed while following. She eyed the table. "Y'all go ahead and sit."

She sat on the opposite end of the table from Mr. Craig. Travis ended up between Jon and Ms. Diane. Brooke went to the chair directly across from him, next to Ms. Diane.

After a long prayer, everyone dug into the feast. There was small chit-chat around the table between the munching and chewing and gulping.

Travis occasionally noticed Brooke glancing towards him. Kelsey, sitting by her cousin, caught Travis peeking at Brooke. Ms. Diane observed it all, but didn't say a word.

"The food is good!" Mr. Craig complimented between bites.

"Mmhmm!" agreed Jon.

The conversation bounced around. They talked about how the softball season ended for the Lady Tigers, and summer league softball for the girls. Travis leaned forward, listening closely to every drill the girls explained. He nodded, as if he could imagine participating in the same work out the softball team had. Then tried to memorize the girl's list of tournaments for the upcoming summer.

"Maybe we can check out some of your games!" Ms. Diane added.

Brooke caught herself smiling at Travis, again.

"What about you, Travis?" Ms. Bridgette asked. "I know they have some summer basketball league. Are you going to play?"

The table quieted. As he began to look around and figure out what to say, Ms. Diane swooped in to save the day, as usual. "Well, hopefully he will be here to play! I know he was saying he's excited about the possibility of playing organized basketball."

For dessert, Mr. Craig pulled out a surprise from the refrigerator. Chocolate banana pudding. At Ms. Diane's encouragement, everyone dove in while he hunted for small bowls and spoons. They left a couple bites for him to enjoy. He chuckled, then shared that he already had a serving while he was in the kitchen! They all laughed, nearly causing Jon to spit out his pudding.

Afterwards, Mr. Craig excused himself and headed to his bedroom for a nap. Jon tried to do the same, but Ms. Diane announced that it was time for the boys to start cleaning.

"The cook doesn't clean," she reminded them. She joined the rest of the girls in the living room to relax. Jon and Travis cleared the dining room table, racking dirty plates and cups into the dishwasher.

The lunch guests were on their way home as the Mooring household prepared for Sunday afternoon naps and NBA basketball on TV. All was well in Travis's new world.

A few days later, the Moorings and Travis drove to meet with the agency representative. The mention of her name seemed to pester Ms. Diane, making her skin crawl. She'd frown, appearing angry with an old nemesis, she seemed serious. The closer they got to Mrs. Brandock's office, the more Ms. Diane appeared aggravated. She complained about traffic. Then not finding a parking spot fast enough. Lastly, about how rude the parking booth man was to them.

"Uh… I can't believe we have to go through this!" Ms. Diane blurted.

Mr. Craig reached over and held his wife's hand. She smiled. The corners of her lips rose just enough to make a semi-circle.

"Was it like this for Jon and Neal and the other boys?" Travis asked.

"Yes… it takes a while. But it will work out," Mr. Craig added. "You have to be patient. Trust, okay?" He had stopped walking, eyes locked into Travis.

Travis nodded his head. *Man, what am I getting myself into? I spent my entire life trying to get out of places, now I'm trying to actually stay put.*

"Don't worry, it'll be okay." Ms. Diane tried to sound cheerful. He couldn't tell who she was trying to encourage more; herself or Travis.

After a couple left turns, right turns, long hallways and waiting areas, he was in the lion's den, face to face with Megan Brandock, behind her desk. An artificial smile and notepad in front of her. Both hands rhythmically playing with an ink pen. Within a few minutes she leaned forward and began the interrogation.

"What's the worst chore that they have forced you to do? Do they fuss and complain when you go to the kitchen? Have you had any fights at school? Do you ever wish you could get away from them? Has Jon ever threatened you or tried to hurt you? Do they buy you stuff just to make you happy? What happened for you to be hospitalized?"

The pace of her questions scared Travis. She would pick up the pen and write for a couple of minutes. Then listen, and write some more.

Should I have said that? Maybe that was wrong. How do I answer that question? Did that make the Moorings sound bad? Do I seem like a bad kid? She must think I'm difficult to live with.

By the time he left her office, he wasn't sure if he should cry or throw a chair through the window. He held himself together until they reached the parking lot. But the second Mr. Craig hit the unlock button on the car remote, flood doors unlocked the water valves.

Ms. Diane spent the next few minutes holding Travis as the tears flowed. "Shh, don't cry, honey." She gently swayed back and forth. "Everything is gonna work out, for whatever is best for you. Just keep believing that no matter what."

"But what if I don't get to stay?" he asked.

"Just worry about doing the best you can and answer her questions truthfully," she replied.

The weekend began with breakfast for dinner; waffles, bacon and hash browns. Travis enjoyed the sight of watching the Moorings laugh and play while cooking together.

As everyone finished eating and prepared to play cards, Ms. Diane's phone rang.

I wonder which one of the boys is calling now, Travis thought.

"Hello?" Ms. Diane had a habit of walking around the house when on the phone.

"Yes, this is she... Okay... Uh-huh... yes... When? Okay... Yes... Okay... Thank you!"

She placed the phone on the counter and hopped around the house full of cheer. "Yes! We have a court date!"

"A court date? Why are you so happy?" Travis was excited but not as joyful.

"That means we passed the first step. Now we're on to the next one," she smiled.

"Which is court," he replied. Then dropped his head.

"And it means we got through one hurdle! The judge will see that as a plus!" Mr. Craig chimed in.

Their court hearing was in two weeks.

What am I gonna do for two weeks? He couldn't handle two weeks of waiting. Not only that, but he had to keep his cool at school and stay out of trouble.

A weekend of basketball, video games and hanging out with Jarel would help. But soon after, it'd be back to the countdown.

Thirteen more days to go. He couldn't handle it. But he soon would learn there was a trustworthy support group around him.

Now if he could avoid doing something stupid, like pushing them away.

Chapter 18

Travis felt he was doing a great job handling the long wait until his court hearing. Although he constantly woke up in cold sweats before the daily 5:45 alarm clock would go off. Some mornings he was up earlier than others – once at 3:45, two other times he was wide awake by 5:00.

While there were daily highs and lows, they all ended in nosedives. Nothing brought joy to him. One day he and Jarel won four games before school. Winning three straight games was challenging enough, especially when seventh or eighth graders snuck onto the court. He smiled after the fourth straight victory. But the joy shook off as the sound of the bell snapped him back to the reminder of the wait.

No matter how much his mind shifted to basketball, school, homework, or a funny joke from Jarel or Brooke, Travis's thoughts quickly returned to court. He tried not to think about it, but all he did was imagine how the hearing would go.

Travis avoided talking about the adoption with everyone – Dean Matts, Jarel, Brooke. His best friend asked him why Travis was acting so strange. But he deflected to testing anxiety and claimed he didn't do well on school tests.

He only asked Jon some simple questions about the process. More detailed inquiries than previously. "Does the adoption become official at court? How often do hearings for foster parents get denied? What type of questions will the judge ask me?"

Plus, Travis was cautious to talk about other things. One day he asked Jon what he should wear to court. The next, he solicited some key words that he should use to help him sound like a good kid in front of the judge. He was smart enough to mix it up. *I don't wanna stress Jon out, he may get mad and decide not to help me.*

His schoolwork improved. In an attempt to keep his mind busy, he picked up reading. Ironic, considered he never made higher than a D in Language Arts. But he followed Ms. Diane's advice and got hooked on some really cool fiction novels. One novel, *Take the Shot*, followed a young kid that loved basketball as much as Travis. He was envious of all the men around the character. As he finished the book he realized that he had people helping him, finally.

Somehow, he also avoided the arch-enemy, Ms. Ranson. While everyone else struggled, he managed to raise his grade in her class to a 'B'.

That will look good at the court hearing when they look at my grades, he thought. *Ah, stop thinking about it!*

Jon disagreed. Travis was constantly knocking at his bedroom door, as predictable as the grandfather clock chiming every hour. Not only did the questions continue, but when Jon answered a question, five new ideas or concerns popped into Travis's head.

As he felt himself become more and more furious with the carousel of questions, Travis would seem content with the answers, and leave. The most frustrating part was Jon's irritated tone and demeanor seemed oblivious to Travis. He was so focused on the court hearing that he didn't realize how tiring the question-and-answer sessions were to Jon.

Although frustrated, he understood what Travis was going through. Jon was in the same position four years prior. Jon Mercado, Court Case #51982. He sat in the same Tuscaloosa courthouse with the Moorings at his side, hopeful the judge would approve his adoption. He remembered the anxiety and fear that swamped his soul as he awaited his final hearing in a warm August courtroom. He recalled stumbling to Neal's room, asking dozens of questions about what the hearings would be like, what it was like to finally belong somewhere. *"What's it feel like to be in a place that the foster parents want you? Do you think they'd want to keep adopting kids after how bad Sherman was?"* Jon shook his head.

Neal had been so patient, careful and honest with his answers. He graciously tolerated Jon's untimely 5:30 visits, which occurred before the alarm clock would go off. Jon knocked heavily in the evenings while Neal was tackling a homework assignment, after spending the afternoon practicing football drills.

"Hey!" Jon remembered yelling through the door frame. *"Can you talk for a minute?"* Jon would wait until he'd hear Neal turn down the music and open the door. He never denied Jon the chance to talk, even if he was jamming out to Christian rap music, a favorite genre that Jon inherited the love for. He also knew the uphill battles awaiting Travis.

"Man, the courts are no joke. They think they care for you, but it's a scary, ugly monster," he remembered Neal saying. Jon hoped, for Travis's sake, and for Ms. Diane and Mr. Craig, that the courts would grant one more break.

Jon knew the Moorings were able to handle whatever mischievous behavior Travis may have stumbled into over the course of the wait. He just wondered how patient Travis would be. He couldn't understand why Travis didn't say anything to Jarel, at least.

Jarel knew something was going on but he couldn't quite figure it out. He thought whatever Travis was dealing with was probably related to the foster situation, hoping that his new best friend would get to stick around. Play summer basketball. Hang out and explore some trails around the county. Maybe visit the mall a couple times and flirt with girls.

He didn't have the same challenges as Travis – his grandparents lived in town. And uncles and aunts now lived in Tuscaloosa. But Jarel had enough friends that went through the foster system that he had an idea of how it went. Plus his friendship with Brooke and Kelsey helped him learn more about foster care. If Travis stayed for summer league, then something good was in the works. He wanted to have Travis permanently in Easton. Not only would the two make a great duo, but Travis was also a pretty cool guy.

They both loved playing video games, playing *real* basketball, and talking about cars. Jarel brought hot rod magazines to school and to the Mooring's house to hang out. After a highly contested series of 1-on-1 games, the two would cool off and renew their friendship by browsing through magazines and point out different features.

Jarel promised Travis that this summer his dad would take him out for a ride in his 1970 Oldsmobile Cutlass Supreme. "P. Daddy", Mr. Pressel's nickname in Garden County, still had a couple small details to polish up on his car before a paint job.

After constantly asking for updates of the car all spring, the questions suddenly ceased. The past two weeks, no more than a three-word sentence could be pulled from Travis.

No matter how silly Jarel was during their bus ride, or how much the boys dominated during their morning basketball games against the best athletes at school, Travis's speech was limited to "good pass" or "nice shot."

Although Jarel missed the usual conversations with Travis, he looked at the silence as an opportunity to talk more trash and to practice his newest and best jokes on bus rides and around school. Travis's quick but accurate facial expressions were enough to let Jarel know if he needed to ditch the joke or pick a better time to use it.

Jarel figured that once testing was over and the school year ended, things would go back to normal. He decided to lay low on pressuring Travis to play summer basketball. But he was curious about how things were going with him and Brooke.

Brooke wondered if she let Travis into her circle of trust too soon. Their friendship changed over the past couple weeks. He blamed it on the stress of the adoption process. She'd been through it before. Adoption and being hurt by guys morphed her sadness into anger.

To think that she trusted him after he tossed her backpack from a speeding bus window was a shock in itself. Kelsey was the first to remind Brooke whenever she commented about Travis's distance over the past couple weeks.

She didn't know why he'd begun acting so different. He hardly spoke to her on the bus, in math class, or anywhere. Maybe he didn't want to get into any more trouble with Mrs.

Ranson, or there was some stipulation on his foster home based on his behavior after the suspension for the fight with George. Was he suffering from late-spring allergies? His medicine could've turned him into a zombie in the mornings.

Since softball season was over, she could hardly get Travis to talk on the bus. It had nothing to do with her finicky cousin Kelsey. Or maybe Travis was so tired of Kelsey that he didn't want to even bother trying to talk to Brooke.

It didn't help that she saw him at church every Sunday. Aunt Bridgette insisted the girls go along with her. Now she would see Travis *six* days a week. Maybe he couldn't handle seeing her *that much*. She thought they had possibly gotten too close. Maybe he thought that Brooke wanted to date, but he wasn't interested in her. *Maybe? Really? Get serious! This is the same punk that threw my backpack out the window!* she thought. Or Travis was falling for her, and was afraid that she wasn't interested in him like that.

Or something happened at his foster home with the Moorings. Was Travis about to move? It didn't make sense for him to get attached to her. She couldn't understand Travis. After a couple days of justifying reasons for his dismissiveness, she had enough. Maybe it was time to get some space between the two.

Brooke wondered if Travis gave Ms. Diane the same silent treatment that he gave her, Jarel and everyone else at school. *She knew how to handle Travis,* Brooke thought.

Ms. Diane was proud of how calm she seemed since receiving the phone call two weeks prior. She managed to maintain her positive and cheerful attitude around Travis.

This was the last time that the Moorings would go through the adoption process. Mr. Craig made it clear before Travis came home. But he also said that when they adopted Neal six years ago.

Regardless of how relaxed she seemed, Ms. Diane was emotionally distraught. Her past with Mrs. Brandock kept replaying in her mind. Every night since their first reunion, she replayed the handshake with Megan's high school teammates and the near scuffle that followed from the back-to-back championship games. As the two girls were separated by teammates, she recalled Megan Brandock pointing and screaming. "I'll get you back! One day!"

Ms. Diane feared that their court date was the day of revenge.

She was surprised how well Travis handled the ups and downs over the past two weeks. The meltdown she feared never came. A shock, considering the earlier incidents since when he first moved in. There was only one phone call from Mrs. Ranson but Ms. Diane didn't worry – Jon, Neal and Sherman all had problems with her.

At home, he was helpful and cordial with Jon, and when he was told to complete chores. He went outside and watched as a family friend brought a road roller over to flatten and even the ground where he and Mr. Craig cleared the previous weeks. She remained hopeful that her own court of dreams would become a reality for Travis.

Her one concern was Travis's increasing, accidental habit, of referring to Ms. Diane as *Mom*. The first time was following the snake bite while he recovered in the hospital. The next month, it slipped a couple times. But as the days went by leading up to the court hearing, he called her *Mom* almost daily.

She wasn't sure if this was due to stress. *Maybe he's reflecting back to his childhood, using names from people when he was a little kid? Or maybe he's really getting that attached to me?* Mr. Craig said little when Ms. Diane mentioned her concerns. They both knew Travis loved his role in the Mooring's home, finally feeling a sense of belonging that could still be taken away.

Since the visit, she noticed Travis coming over to her room or meandering around her in the kitchen more often. He desired her presence and approval more and more. It was like she had a four-year-old – she couldn't sneak away for a bathroom break!

Travis didn't realize the impact he had on people around him.

But today it was all about him. His nerves were more rattled than he could have ever imagined. Legs wobbly like Jell-O, he slipped trying to climb into Mr. Craig's truck.

When they arrived at the courthouse, Travis found Lincoln dressed in a white shirt with a blue and gray tie. He couldn't remember seeing him dressed up. His joy quickly faded as he noticed Mrs. Brandock standing next to Lincoln. Ms. Diane seemed relieved when her foe greeted her with a big hug and smile.

As Travis walked into the downtown courthouse with his team of adults, his mind flashed back to the first time he appeared in court. Only eight years old, soon after the explosion at Smiley Court Apartments that killed his mother Cheryl Johns and Uncle Eddy.

He remembered how nervous and scared he was. He had no idea where he was going or what really happened to his mother and uncle. He didn't know what foster care was or what his future foster home would look like, or the foster parent would care for Travis.

His memories changed into nightmares at the sight of familiar and unwanted faces: Kage and Kedrick. Two of his four nemesis from the torturous time in Hoover. The two giant smiles replaced the saddened frowns they wore before recognizing him.

He tried to lead the adults to sit on the right side of the aisle. It worked, but they escorted him around to a row in front of the two boys. He heard whispers close to his right ear.

"Travy! Travy" He knew who it was. But he turned his head in their direction anyway. Kage held his hands together, then pretended to swing an imaginary pillow. He knew what was intended.

Pillow-tag. Even in court, Travis couldn't escape his past.

But he was quickly reminded that this time his life was much different. As despair began to flood his soul, he felt Ms. Diane wrap her arm around and pull him in close to her. His safety net was here. So was the judge.

"All rise for the honorable Judge O'Neal!" instructed the bailiff.

It was time. Game time.

Chapter 19

Everyone rose in the courtroom. An old, large black man with a limp strolled in. Through the thin-rimmed glasses, the judge's face seemed stoic. He looked like he had suffered a heartbreaking loss on the basketball court in a senior league game. His presence, size and stature, mirrored old NBA star, Bill Russell.

Judge O'Neal looked over the top of his glasses as Travis Mitchell was called forward. The Moorings followed, closely behind. Lincoln Arnold and Megan Brandock both pulled up the rear. They whispered unclear phrases to each other. The only words clear were *"oh, no."*

"Quite a detailed report, Mrs. Brandock." Judge O'Neal looked over a document, then flipped pages while talking to himself. "Good morning to you all, Mr. and Mrs. Mooring and Mr. Mitchell."

"Good morning," they all replied.

"And good morning, young lad," Judge O'Neal faced Lincoln and smiled.

"Hello, Judge O'Neal," Lincoln said, as serious as Travis had ever seen him. More so than when he warned Travis not to mess things up with the Moorings.

"Mr. Mitchell," the judge began. "How have you fared living with the Moorings?"

Travis was unsure how to reply. *Do I tell the truth? Does he already know about all the trouble I got into with them?* He looked around then back at the judge.

He thought about the first time he went onto the dirt court to shoot. It hadn't seemed like much in the past. Oh man, what he'd give to be there now, in the solitude. Hear the exaggerated pound of the ball on compacted dirt, the orange worn-out ball ricochet off the backboard and rattle around through the faded rim. Listen to the ball scratch through the chains.

Travis thought about how impressed he was with Ms. Diane's ability to shoot. How little he knew about her and Mr. Craig until he started to realize he wanted to be there. About how amazing the Moorings really had been to him. He looked back at the intimidating Judge O'Neal, swallowed, and took a deep breath.

"Well, Judge, honestly, it's been amazing, unbelievable. I mean, Ms. Diane and Mr. Craig have really been great. They're really smart. It's like, they don't do what you would expect them to do."

Judge O'Neal leaned forward. He nodded, then spun his hand in small, quick circular motions. Travis assumed this meant to continue.

"It's like they're already inside my head. It's good, but frustrating at the same time." Travis paused. He needed to clarify. "When I said *inside my head*, I mean that they have some crazy punishment that's nothing like I'd expect. Or they'll say something that gets to the problem. Or when I'm upset, they say something that makes me feel good and important. Afterward, I'll lay in bed and I think "*How'd she know to say that?*" or "*How did he know to do that?*" After I while, I realized that they were what I needed in my life. They just make me wanna do better."

His head lowered, angled at the table in front of him. He feared that he said too much, or the wrong thing, or something that would make the Moorings look like unfit foster parents.

"Is that so?" Judge O'Neal rubbed his chin. His eyes slowly brightened, the corners of his lips rose.

Travis took another deep breath before letting it out. "It's no secret about some of the problems I've had at school. But Ms. Diane and Mr. Craig, they just deal with it differently. They don't yell or scream or act crazy. They just talk to me. The consequences always fit the crime. It's like they've done this before." He turned toward Ms. Diane and smiled.

"Ah, so you've learned something!" Judge O'Neal interlocked his fingers as if he was preparing to pray.

"Yes sir," Travis hesitated. "They really want to take care of me. It just took me a while to realize it."

"Hmm." The judge turned his chair slightly to face Mr. Craig and Ms. Diane. "Mr. and Mrs. Mooring, do you two understand the responsibility and commitment for supervising, guiding, mentoring, providing for, and caring for Travis?"

"Yes, your honor," they both replied, almost in unison.

"Do you understand the accountability legally, morally, financially and physically that you are accepting for the remainder of Travis Mitchell's adolescence?"

Again, they answered in unison. "Yes, your Honor."

He continued, "In the records, I notice that Travis will be the fifth young man that you have gone through adoption hearings for?"

"Yes sir." Ms. Diane's proud and loving voice overshadowed Mr. Craig for the first time.

"Mm-hmm. And the other young men are doing well?"

"Yes, sir." Both answered.

"How so?"

Mr. Craig took the lead, "The first person we adopted was Tyreese Pong. He graduated from Garden County High School and played basketball at Louisiana Tech. He is now teaching and coaching high school basketball in St. Louis."

He looked up at Judge O'Neal who nodded, as if asking Mr. Craig to continue. "Sherman Hampton was next. He came to us while Tyreese was a junior in high school. Sherman is living in Memphis now. He also graduated from Garden County High School and is a senior at the University of Memphis. Once he graduates he is going to join the military. He loves working with electronics." His tone sounded proud, as if he enjoyed bragging about his boys. His inner-dad was slowly coming out.

"Neal Douglas was next. We adopted him a few years later. He recently graduated from Garden County High School and is on a football scholarship at Mount Union College. They're a small Division 3 school in Ohio. Neal is a sophomore there."

"The most recent finalized adoption was Jon Mercado. A lot of names to keep up with!" Mr. Craig chuckled, trying to catch his breath.

"Jon is a junior in high school. He's doing well in school and at home. He stays busy with football and weightlifting," Ms. Diane added. "We don't force any of the kids to play, but we have noticed that sports serves as a great coping mechanism for the boys. It's like their therapy, a release. A safe place to burn off the frustration from the obstacles they faced when they were younger."

Mr. Craig quickly glanced at Ms. Diane. Then faced Judge O'Neal while bowing his head. The judge nodded in approval.

"I guess Mr. Mitchell has a sport, too. Is that accurate?"

"Yes sir. I love basketball," Travis answered. "I hope to play summer league for my school next month."

"Mhm. Mr. Arnold, stand please. What are your thoughts?"

"Yes, sir." He cleared his throat, then fidgeted with his tie to make sure it was straightened. "I believe that Travis would do well with placement with Mr. Craig and Mrs. Diane Mooring. Travis struggled early. But we know that's common. In my history with Travis, he has been the happiest and has also showed the most growth with the Moorings."

"Yes, I see in your notes, Mr. Arnold. I appreciate it." Judge O'Neal continued flipping through the stack of papers. "Mrs. Brandock, any final comments that you wish to share?"

"Yes, your honor." She quickly glanced at Ms. Diane. Travis could hear the air empty from Ms. Diane's soul.

"I did address some concerns of Travis's behavior at school and the necessity of law enforcement to be involved. This includes an incident that resulted in a snake bite. Travis was hospitalized. However, there seems to be a change of behavior for the better, in the past month. I'd like to conduct further follow-up interviews with school administrators and others to collect information before finalizing. Maybe consider waiting a little longer."

"Thank you for sharing." Judge O'Neal frowned, his eyes seemed to penetrate Travis's mind. "I'll agree to follow-up interviews with school personnel regarding Mr. Mitchell before we make a final decision. I'm puzzled why this interview wasn't conducted prior to this hearing. We'd be able to move to the next steps."

Mrs. Brandock lowered her head. Hands fidgeted on the table. She seemed nervous. Before she had a chance to answer, the judge continued.

"Nonetheless, this is one of the more encouraging hearings in my courtroom. The history of Mr. and Mrs. Mooring with foster children is commendable. Approval is pending. We'll set a final hearing in two weeks from today."

Wham!

The judge slammed his gavel. Travis's group was ushered out of the courtroom. It was all gibberish to Travis. The words he yearned to hear didn't come. At least not today.

Good news, you get to wait. For two more weeks. As if I haven't waited enough! Travis squeezed the top of his chair then paused. Slamming it under the table would be a terrible mistake. Slowly, he pushed the wooden seat in. Then walked down the aisle towards heavy, oak doors. He couldn't bring himself to look up to see Kage and Kedrick chuckle.

"Where were you this morning?" Brooke asked. The bell rang, setting Mrs. Ranson's math class free from her overbearing presence.

"Court stuff," Travis replied, mundanely.

"Oh, ok." Brooke clutched the straps of her backpack and pulled her hands together. "For custody, placement stuff?"

Travis nearly looked in shock. Then tried to play it off. *How did she know?*

"Yes, that boring-type stuff," Travis answered nonchalantly.

"Cool, bro. But Ms. Diane made you come to school afterward?" Jarel chimed in. He strolled next to him, then rested his arm on his friend's shoulder.

"Yes, dude," Travis turned around. "You know how she is. I think she had to go into work, anyway."

"Well, you missed watching me tear it up in PE! We played wiffleball," Jarel continued.

"You?" Brooke gave Jarel a playful shove.

"Okay, I had some help," he clarified. "Brooke chased down some deep hits. I almost confused her with a softball player." Jarel's voice level rose and fell as Brooke swung an open hand to smack him again. "So, any news?" He tried to change the topic.

"On… what?" said Travis.

"Come on, you're not gonna tell your closest bud?"

Travis didn't know what to say. He hoped to keep people from talking about it. And he didn't want to say anything until it was official.

"He's not ready to talk about it," Brooke snapped. She then turned to Travis and smiled, "We'll just pray about it."

"Pray that he doesn't lose that jump shot, too!" Jarel joked.

Right now, anything will be helpful, Travis thought.

Halfway through a quiet spaghetti and meatball dinner, Travis finally broke the silence. "So now what? We just wait for another hearing? To have a hearing to decide the next hearing?"

Ms. Diane put her fork down and wiped her mouth. She patted Travis's hand gently. "Did I tell you how sweet that was to hear you say those nice things about us?" She added. "Almost brought tears to my eyes!"

Travis looked away. He meant every word he said, but right now his concern was how the court hearings would end up.

"It's a big step forward," Mr. Craig added.

"A court date to have another court date?" Travis challenged. "That's just stupid."

"It is. But it gives you two more weeks to make sure this is what you want." Ms. Diane tried to sound cheerful.

"Or, you can spend the next couple of weeks researching how to pave the court," Mr. Craig added.

Travis turned around towards the back yard, where the land had been leveled.

"Are you thinking what I'm thinking?" Ms. Diane asked. Travis smiled.

Ms. Diane and Travis headed outside. Mr. Craig turned, faced Jon and frowned.

"Let's go you lazy bums!" she yelled, then grabbed her Nikes from the bedroom. "I guess I'll take Travis on my team, even though he can't shoot like me!"

Earlier today, Travis could only dream of spending time on the dirt court. Now, he got the best medicine for any illness he could imagine- a nighttime basketball game outside. Although he loved Mr. Craig's idea of a paved court, this was something he could get used to.

Chapter 20

During breakfast, Ms. Diane recommended a change from the typical weekend plans for Travis. "It'd be nice for you to have a fun day, get away from all the stress."

"Like what?" Travis asked between gulps of orange juice.

"Craig and I were planning to run errands in town. We could take you, Jarel and the girls up there. You guys can do arcades, bowling or something, maybe catch a movie. I think Ms. Bridgette works today. I'm sure she wouldn't mind if we brought the girls along, but it's up to you."

"Yeah. Yes, ma'am. That'd be cool. Watching Jarel bother Kelsey is good entertainment," Travis laughed.

"Okay! Call Jarel and I'll call Ms. Bridgette." She hustled on as Mr. Craig returned home from dropping off Jon for a football competition.

"Are we going to town?" Mr. Craig sounded really enthusiastic for someone about to go to the mall, a fabric store, and shop for a new dishwasher. He came into the kitchen and headed straight for the coffee pot.

"Yup!" Travis answered. He dialed Jarel's phone number.

Within the hour, Ms. Diane's grey Expedition was transformed into a school bus, without the school part. As they pulled onto the highway, Ms. Diane shared the plans for the day with Travis' newly appointed riding partners.

"I figure we can check out the Alabama Museum of Natural History, first. Then y'all can go to the arcade or something," she began.

"Di, really? You want to drag these kids to more school stuff?" Mr. Craig asked.

"Honey, it'll be fun and free!" She turned around and smiled at Travis. "Anyway, we don't have to stay too long."

"With all due respect, Ms. Diane," Jarel began, "history isn't my favorite subject. I mean, I barely remember when my *birthday* is!" He sat with Travis in the third row. He leaned forward to speak, resting his arms between Kelsey and Brooke's seats.

"Haha! I can't help you on that, but you can see the dinosaur exhibits and animals."

"Maybe we can leave him as an exhibit." Kelsey nudged Jarel's arms off the seat. "We can make a booth titled *Animal with a brain smaller than a dinosaur.*"

Ah, let the trash-talking begin.

It continued for a few more minutes before Mr. Craig turned up the radio. It was a silent method to let the two middle schoolers know it was time to be quiet.

As the bunch strolled through the museum, Travis felt slightly nervous around Brooke. Fortunately, Jarel was close enough to say or do something, causing everyone to laugh with him or at Kelsey.

Travis was fascinated to see the different exhibits. Not really a dinosaur fan since his youth, the deinosuchus rugosus interested him. A giant crocodile that grew as large as thirty-nine feet long.

Slow strolls throughout the museum, pointing at different dinosaurs and animals as the group travelled through the centuries made Travis ponder. He loved to see how animals changed, and the evolution of civilization for humans.

Ms. Diane magically transformed Travis into a history-lover. He wasn't sure if it was naturally, or because he yearned to know about his own family.

Once Travis and the kids were dropped off at the bowling alley, Jarel began to really act up. Ms. Diane instructed they had a couple hours to hang out and get lunch. She adamantly warned Jarel and Kelsey that she was to be told where they were and what they were doing. Travis had never seen her so serious. The look from his friends indicated they were fearful of any consequence she would issue, even if they didn't live with her.

The foursome bowled a couple games. Jarel won both in a landslide. He continued to taunt Kelsey and Travis as they returned their shoes while the girls considered lunch ideas.

"I see a basketball shooting game in the corner," Travis said, with a devilish grin. Jarel's shooting arm was a bit fatigued from bowling, unlike his mouth.

"Man, come on. You're not trying to lose to me again. In front of the girls?" Jarel buffed.

Brooke stopped her conversation with Kelsey to listen.

"I'm betting on Travis," Brooke added. "You're not gonna chicken out, are you Jarel? I'm sure you've got one more victory in you!" She smiled as Kelsey joined in.

"Hurry up! I'm hungry!" Kelsey hollered.

"Hush woman! I'll make this beating as quick or slow as I like!" Jarel began walking towards the basketball goals. "I would've beat y'all in half the time bowling if you didn't keep getting gutter balls and jamming the machine. Come on Travis! Come and taste defeat, again!"

Both boys entered their coins as the sticky, rubber basketballs rolled down from behind the gate. Highest score in sixty seconds would be the winner.

It took ten seconds before either hit a shot. Kelsey was quick to remind them of how bad they were shooting.

Finally Travis got hot, hitting six shots in a row. Then Jarel had a nice streak of makes. At the halfway point, Travis led 12-8. The girls were cheering. Mainly, Brooke cheered. Kelsey booed both as the countdown reached fifteen seconds. The lead flip-flopped with every made shot.

Jarel was up 18-17 with ten seconds left. With eight ticks left, Travis took the lead 20-19. Four seconds, Jarel was up 22-21.

Three… two… one… tied 23-23, Travis let loose his last shot. It rattled through the chains and rubbed the sensor tallying points just before the buzzer sounded. Both looked down as Travis's scoreboard changed to 24.

"Yes! Good shot, Travis!" Brooke yelled. She wrapped her arms around his neck from behind while hopping up and down. It was a celebratory choking. The boys were shocked with the buzzer-beater, and Brooke's reaction.

"Now we don't have to hear Jarel talk trash anymore." Brooke tried to downplay her excitement. "Right?"

"Last-second shot. Nothing sweeter!" Travis tried to move past Brooke's moment.

"You won a game that doesn't even count." Jarel shrugged, then walked towards the food court.

"What's the beginning of the sentence?" Travis asked. "Was it *'You beat me'*? That's all that counts."

"Let's get a group picture before lunch," Brooke recommended. Reluctantly, Jarel agreed. "Over here, by the scoreboard," she chuckled.

Jarel frowned, while Kelsey and Travis laughed. Brooke asked a lady near them to take a couple photos while she squeezed between Travis and Kelsey. Jarel stood on the other side of Travis, but kept his arms crossed.

"Come on, I want a good picture." Brooke leaned forward, demanding. "This lady doesn't have time to wait on you."

Jarel complied. After a couple of pictures, Brooke instructed Travis to take the camera and snap some shots of the girls. As he prepared to snap a photo, a text message flashed onto the screen. "Looks like our mom-for-the-day is checking in." Travis said while holding the phone away from his face.

"Yup." Jarel pulled his phone out of his pocket. It flashed. Seemed like Ms. Diane forwarded her message to both of them. "And I'm going to tell her that Kelsey was being bad!"

"Let's hurry up and get some food." Brooke read Ms. Diane's message. "She said we have thirty minutes to eat before they get here to pick us up."

Travis was grateful to get away from the stress of court, a break from worrying over the results of the next hearing. He couldn't recall any time he hung out with friends at other foster homes. He was ready to get the week underway and countdown to Friday. Well, a *week* from *next* Friday.

Tuesday included a surprise visit from Lincoln at school. Travis happened to walk through the office with Jarel to visit Dean Matts. He intended to find summer basketball forms.

Travis saw Lincoln waiting outside the principal's office with Megan Brandock. Neither said a word. This was supposed to be an "unknown visit" for the case worker. He knew why the two were there. To speak with Dean Matts, the principal, the counselor and some other teachers. Hopefully not Mrs. Ranson. It'd be all over if that happened.

Later that evening, Ms. Diane received a phone call from Mrs. Brandock. Travis couldn't hear much, but stared intently.

Once he realized who was on the phone, he watched her body language and facial expressions.

"She said everything looks good with the updated notes." Ms. Diane paused. "She also said that the final court hearing *could* be moved up, but wasn't certain when."

Travis leaped, then jumped into Ms. Diane's arms. With the same energy and excitement as Brooke hopped onto his back after his victory over Jarel. Like Kobe Bryant flew into Shaq's giant arms after the duo won their first NBA championship.

Ms. Diane spent the rest of the week avoiding Travis any time her phone rang. He followed her throughout the house and stared, trying to determine if she was speaking to a case worker or one of her friends. Unfortunately, there was no call. Another week full of hope, only to end with more waiting. By Friday morning, Travis, and the whole Mooring household was barely holding on.

"Beach getaway this weekend." Mr. Craig said. Everyone rushed in and out of the kitchen. They all moved with enough pace to survive a Friday morning.

"What?" Jon asked. He sat in the dining room, lacing up his dark grey Durant shoes.

"Spanish Fort, this weekend. Family trip," Mr. Craig repeated.

"Yeah?" Ms. Diane said as she walked to the kitchen, putting on her earrings. "Sounds like a fun idea. You boys have anything going on this weekend?"

"Nothing I can't skip," Jon smiled.

"Have your bags packed by 5pm!" Mr. Craig stated, smiling at Travis.

Travis wasn't thrilled at the idea but appreciated what the Moorings were trying to do. He gave Mr. Craig a nonchalant high-five, and grabbed his backpack. Then headed to the bus stop with Jon.

By the time their Expedition pulled into the hotel parking lot at Spanish Fort, it was already dark. The weary bunch checked into their rooms and stumbled up the stairway to their second-floor suite.

"I'll wake y'all up early so we can see the sunrise. It'll be worth it!" Ms. Diane said as the boys entered in their room.

"Ugh, really?" the boys both replied.

"If you really don't enjoy it, then I won't get you up early on Sunday," she negotiated.

Of course Ms. Diane was right. Travis enjoyed the gentle sound of waves withering as they splashed onto the shore. Mid-way through an early stroll on the beach, he reminisced about the only beach trip he took with his mom.

It was actually Uncle Eddy and his girlfriend, Emily. They brought Travis along. He recalled a weary sunrise walk. Each adult held one of the then-eight year-old's tiny hands, swinging him high into the sky. He remembered times when he would jokingly tell Emily that she was his "*pretend mommy*." He vaguely recollected wondering what it'd be like to live with Uncle Eddy and Emily. He thought about their getaway and its timely impact. The beach trip occurred a weekend before the explosion at the apartment. A sudden end to his uncle and mother's lives.

As he began to feel overwhelmed, Ms. Diane grabbed his arm with one hand and Jon with her other, pulling both boys close to her.

"My two babies," she exclaimed. "Enjoying a beautiful sunrise with the two boys that bring joy to my life!"

"Come on, Ms. Diane," Jon frowned.

She released Jon's arm and grabbed him around the neck. Then pulled him down to her level as she stood on her tiptoes and smacked a kiss on the cheek. She did the same to Travis.

"Y'all are my babies," she continued. "I love you two!"

Travis enjoyed the getaway. He had crab legs and fell in love at first bite, or snap. They all played putt-putt later and went to a seafood restaurant for dinner. Ms. Diane, by favorable score-keeping, won their putt-putt game. In the evening, the adults lounged on beach chairs while Jon and Travis enjoyed the ocean.

As much fun as Travis had, he was ready to get back home and speed on to Friday. His court date with the judge was coming.

"Hey, guys." Dean Matts greeted as the boys got off their bus Monday morning.

"What's up, Dean?" Jarel replied, then slapped hands.

"Travis, you got a minute?" Dean Matts asked. It sounded less like a question, more like a gentle demand.

"Yes sir?" Travis answered. Jarel headed towards the basketball court.

"I know things are still up in the air, but I think it may be a good idea to do the paperwork for summer league." Travis frowned. "I get it. You still don't know what's going to happen. But best case scenario, you'll be ready."

"It doesn't make sense to do paperwork just to hear that I'll be going somewhere else!" Travis realized he was a little louder than he needed to be.

Dean Matts paused before continuing. "I gotcha. I'm not trying to stir up the issue. I think you're in a good position. Thinking positive is easy to say but not to do, so I'm challenging you to actually *do* it."

As the week wound down, Travis's frustration rose. His demeanor changed from quiet and worried, to angry and bitter. It was evident to others on the bus ride home Thursday afternoon.

"What up, man? What are you stressing over?" Jarel asked.

"Nothing, dude." Travis sat, facing forward.

"You sure?"

"Yeah, it's cool." Travis dropped his head. Then added, "Court hearing is tomorrow, after I was told it was gonna be moved up, but never was."

"Oh. You wanna talk about it?"

Travis was tired of talking about it and the motivational pep talks from everyone about the court hearing. He was tired of Mo... Ms. Diane, and Mr. Craig and Dean Matts and Jon. Everyone already knew what was on his mind. He didn't need any reminders.

Plus, he got in trouble in Ms. Ranson's class earlier. That only added fuel to the fire. He was sure he'd have ISD on Friday, after he received bad news from the hearing.

"Don't sweat it." Brooke leaned forward. "I know it'll work out. I know how you feel." He partially turned around in shock. It was like Brooke knew his story. "Didn't I tell you this is a small place? You have a bad memory!" She smiled and patted his shoulder. Then sat back.

"Hey, you heard her! There are three women in Garden County that I would always listen to. Kelsey isn't one, well I guess she is. Anyone who hates guys that much *has* to be a woman." Jarel chuckled. "Anyway, the three women I'd listen to: my mom because she'd beat me, Ms. Diane. She'd beat anyone, except me because I'm her favorite. And Brooke, she's smart and will get Kelsey to beat me up."

He fidgeted in his seat, then faced Travis. "That list is the women I'd listen to in *Garden County*. If Michelle Obama or Kerry Washington came, I'd listen to them too!"

"You are so dumb!" Kelsey yelled.

"She's one to talk," Jarel whispered. "She's right. I forgot about…"

"I will go upside your head if you start with a fantasy list!" Kelsey pulled her hand back, preparing to swing.

"If you don't put that hand down!" Mrs. Rachel looked into her mirror.

"Oh my gosh! I love you so much! Thank you for saving my life, again!" Jarel screamed.

"Be quiet before I get both of yall's moms up here!" she barked.

Travis laughed at Jarel and his silly antics.

"Don't worry. It'll all work out," Brooke whispered to him.

"Yeah man," Jarel added. "It's like my dad says to me, '*Heads down, prayers up*.'"

It sounded catchy, but what Travis really wanted to hear is 'The adoption is approved.' He was going to hear something, one way or another, soon enough.

Chapter 21

"We aren't taking you to court with us tomorrow," Ms. Diane stated as they finished dinner. "You're going to school in the morning. We will let you know when we find out the ruling."

More words and phrases followed. None that he cared to listen to. He was beside himself that he wasn't allowed to go hear for himself. It was *his life.*

In the same breath, Travis knew that he was being selfish. The judge's verdict would impact the Moorings as much as him. He thought about the famous Jackie Robinson quote that Mr. Pressel shared one evening:

"A life is not important except for its impact on other lives."

He believed he'd made a positive impact on the Moorings, Jarel, Jon, Brooke, and even Kelsey in the short time he'd been in Easton. But this didn't detract from the point that he should be at the hearing.

Friday morning, he planned to oversleep so he'd be late for school. *That'll force Ms. Diane and Mr. Craig to bring me to court.*

Somehow Jon knew the plan. He barged into Travis's room a few minutes after the alarm clock buzzed, then warned, "Don't bother trying. It won't work out. Of all days to try something, this isn't the day. Ms. Diane won't fall for it." His pep-talk continued, "She'll risk being a no-show at court just to take you to school. And that'll definitely get the judge's ruling that none of us want. So get up and get ready." He closed the door. Then came back. "And don't do anything stupid at school. Just because the ink is on the paper, it's not final. It can still change, for the worse."

Travis slumped in his seat on the bus. Sat with his arms crossed, eyebrows scrunched. His friends were surprised to see him this morning.

"You're not going to court?" Jarel asked.

"I'm not. They are." Travis snapped.

"No sweat," Brooke tried to cheer.

Travis slouched, refrained from saying anything snappy to Brooke. Their friendship had come so far since the backpack incident, she seemed to trust him.

Dean Matts spoke to Travis for a minute when he got off the bus. Apparently Ms. Diane sent him a message the day before to let him know their plans. "My office is open. I know you've got a lot going on, especially today. You can just hang out in ISD for a while, help avoid any problems in class."

Travis's body language morphed from bad to worse. Wrinkles popped onto his forehead. "No, I'm good." He thought about one of the many lessons on patience the Moorings taught him. "Never mind. Can I come for the second half of school, after lunch? You know how Mrs. Ranson is."

Dean Matts nodded with approval, proud of the decision that everyone knew was best. Glad Travis quickly reversed his stance and acknowledged. "See you after lunch."

Making it to the halfway point would be a challenge.

After their brief talk, Travis headed to the basketball court. He and George nearly got into another scuffle. This time it was clear that Travis was the instigator.

Jarel pulled Travis back, spun him around, and then got in his face. "Chill," he shouted. "Don't be stupid, man! He ain't worth it!"

"Doesn't matter if I whip him again!" Travis yelled. "I won't be here long anyway!"

"Yo, think about Ms. Diane! You want her to get a call from school, while she's in front of the judge?" He held Travis back. "You don't know what blessing is happening there. Relax!"

Travis made it through his first couple of classes and lunch without any other incidents. During Language Arts, he pretended to follow along to the class readings about John Henry. *Folk tales. Fake stories. What's the point? A happy ending that didn't really happen?* He looked up in time to see Ms. Raney walking towards his table. Tall, black, and fiercely gentle. She didn't say much. Simply patted his shoulder. Travis dropped his head. Her silence affirmed the need for him to detach from the court case. She'd purposely chosen this book because of his love for history, he found out earlier in the week.

Fortunately, a friend was in each class to help him get through the morning. Jarel, Brooke, or Kelsey were sure to speak to him before each class leading up to lunch. A team effort to help him out.

"Yo, Dean Matts! I'm placing Travis in your care! Keep him safe, okay?" Jarel joked as lunch ended.

"Yeah, okay," Dean Matts commented. He paid little attention to Jarel.

"I'm serious… sir," he added, not wanting to push his luck. "Actually, I think I need to go, too. I've been having problems in class on Friday afternoons."

"Oh? Well that's an easy fix." He reached into his pocket, then pulled out his cell phone. "Should I call your dad at the shop or your mom at the high school?"

"Hah…. Uh, haha! Man, you know what, I think the problem disappeared!" Jarel chortled. "You know what, I'm gonna go grab that work for Travis and bring it by *after* school. See you later!"

Travis spent the remainder of the day bouncing between the dean's office and adjacent ISD room. He worked on an assignment for Science. Created a neat project on teaching the water cycle to kindergartners. Dean Matts vanished every fifteen minutes.

"Sheesh, these folks keep you busy," Travis commented. He walked into Dean Matts's office as two students moped down the hall.

"Like you guys say, everyone is always trippin!" Dean Matts threw his hands in the air like he was giving up.

Travis laughed as the office phone rang.

"Dean Matts. Okay, yup… Really? Okay. Yes he's here now. Thanks… I'll send him up."

"What's up?" Travis asked.

Dean Matts rocked in his chair, then spoke gently. "Well, usually I don't tell others' business, but I'll share since it involves you. Mr. Craig is in the office to check you out. Lucky you… getting to leave early."

Travis shrugged and pointed at the clock, "Big deal. It's only ten minutes before the bell rings."

"Still early, right?" He smiled, then stood. "Hope you have a great weekend."

"You mean a great life?" Travis grabbed his backpack and headed out.

Travis wasn't too happy to see Mr. Craig. He nodded as he walked by him in the front office and headed out to the truck.

The wise old man paid no attention to Travis. Watched the youngster walk out the building, then talked to the lady at the front desk.

"So you know, I haven't heard the final decision is. The judge had more questions." Mr. Craig unlocked the door. "I figured we can get some stuff done today. Keep our minds free."

"Like what? Get some boxes or suitcases?"

"First is your physical. We made an appointment for today a few weeks ago. It crept up on us. That's why we didn't bring you this morning. Didn't want you to miss more school."

"Okay." Travis didn't care what excuse spewed. He wanted to be done so he could go back home. Home… *I haven't called a place home since forever. The only 'home' I knew was Smiley Court Apartments. That wasn't even home, that was dysfunction.* Never in his life had he admitted to himself that the upbringing that Cheryl Johns provided was hectic, terrible. Honestly, Cheryl didn't provide anything. The only person that had ever cared for him was Uncle Eddy. He made sure Travis was taken care of, fed, clothed, and taught. And Cheryl, *"Mom,"* tragically took him away. She chose something else over her own son. Her addiction to drugs had ruined lives– Travis and Uncle Eddy's to start with. Emily, too. All Cheryl had to do was be unselfish and let Uncle Eddy be Travis' legal guardian. But she wanted the money, to put herself first. Get her next fix. Now Travis was the one who lost. Everything.

Travis was so deep in his thoughts, he hardly noticed Mr. Craig on the phone. He figured it was probably Ms. Diane. Travis mulled the reality of his life. *Why me? Why did all this happen to me? What'd I do to deserve this?*

After the physical, they stopped at a hardware store. Mr. Craig led with long strides. Then paused along multiple aisles. He looked grabbed a pair of rubber boots and picked up two weird flat tools. One had a handle but the front was flat. The other looked like an industrial broom with a wide, flat bottom. He recommended they stop and grab dinner before heading home.

Mr. Craig suggested a seafood restaurant that some of his co-workers suggested. "I heard they have really good crab legs."

"Okay," Travis reluctantly agreed.

Friday nights were their fun family meal. Game nights. At least for a little while longer. Travis couldn't bring himself to talk.

Neither did Mr. Craig. No one wanted to talk about the hearing earlier in the day. Travis heard enough when he was picked him up from school.

Travis's thought about past doom, misery, and future misfortune so deeply, he fell asleep on the way home. He woke up as they inched up the dirt driveway.

As Mr. Craig shifted the truck into park, Travis hopped out the truck without his backpack. "I'm gonna shoot for a little bit." More of a statement than asking for permission.

"Okay, the ball should still be out back," Mr. Craig said. He climbed down and headed towards the front door as Travis walked around the house. He didn't realize how dark the house was- he was focused on shooting and getting to his happy place.

Great, where's the ball? I left it by the goal yesterday. He steamed, then peeked in the barn. No ball. He took long strides towards the back porch with his head down. *Need to get these weeds cut*, he thought.

It wasn't until Travis was halfway to the back steps when he stopped. *What's that?* He saw a wheelbarrow with a dozen bags of what looked like concrete mix. The hose unwound, laying nearby. 2x4's piled up. *What is that for? The court? No more dirt cou...* Before he finished thinking, he walked up the steps.

A huge, white banner hung the length of the porch.

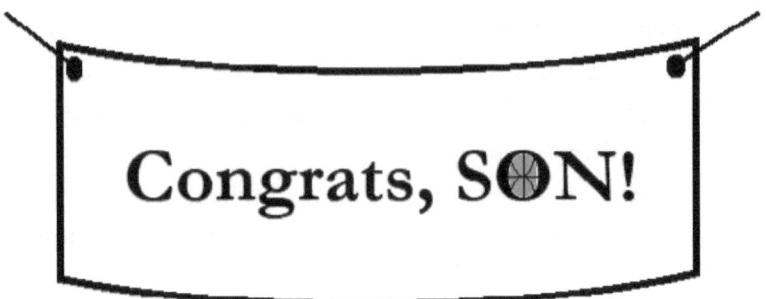

The 'o' in *SON* looked like a basketball. Balloons in different colors hung throughout the porch. Red, yellow, and orange. Colors of the local high school and a basketball.

He couldn't think. He looked at the sign again. There were written notes taped on the door from different people. Kelsey, Jarel, Brooke, Dean Matts, Jon. Then a short note from Mr. Craig and longer one from Ms. Diane. There was even a message from Lincoln and Mrs. Brandock taped to the window.

Travis sat down. Then cried. *Home, for good.*

After a few seconds, all the lights in the house instantly flickered on. He was greeted by a loud, "Congratulations!" from the top of everyone's lungs.

Ms. Diane was the first one out. "Welcome home, son!" She embraced him. They sobbed, holding each other.

Everyone Travis knew followed. They were all jammed inside, waiting for his grand arrival. She ushered her newest son inside. A huge cake was positioned in the dining room.

Jarel got a hold of Travis after a few minutes. "So, back to that summer league deal, I heard you already got the physical." The boys smiled.

Next issue to tackle: summer league championship. But first, upgrading the dirt court. Travis turned back, then squeezed the Moorings, Ms. Diane in one arm and Mr. Craig in the other. *Permanent court. Permanent home.*

About the Author

Johnny Bell was born in Fayetteville, North Carolina. He spent the first ten years of his life bouncing around the country with his family living on different military bases. During his early childhood, he met a vast array of classmates and friends. Each relationship led to new experiences and exposed the dynamics of different homes and families. His posse included a friend that loved video games but lived in a single-parent household, another with two brothers that were as opposite as black and white, and a girl with the greatest athletic ability he had ever seen. She was the first one picked for every kickball game. Every. Single. Time. By the time he settled into a small, north-Florida city, he had experienced enough to write a book. But there was still more to learn! Johnny befriended peers that lived on both sides of the railroad tracks. During this time, he realized that life is not as easy as it may appear. Some buddies in suburbia were dealing with divorce and violence in their homes while other classmates at school were growing up in the hood with a loving parent and good meals.

Johnny has grown his collection of published work – first with *Take the Shot* and now with *The Dirt Court*. Prior to publication, one of his former students focused her Black History Research piece on Johnny's contributions and accomplishments as an educator. He prides himself in utilizing the experiences and memories from interactions with the hundreds of students he has mentored and supervised over the last fifteen years. The accuracy of basketball drills and sequence of events are a credit to the twelve seasons he spent coaching boys' high school basketball.

During his time roaming the sidelines, Johnny was part of three Regional Finalist teams and one that advanced to the state's Final Four tournament. Johnny volunteered at various college basketball camps across the state, learning different drills, techniques, and coaching strategies. Most important was building strong relationships with players and helping them strive to become positive and productive young men in society.

Johnny's experience as an educator has vastly come into play. His passion for writing is purely to share the tales and ordeals that students are struggling with. It is an untold story of managing "a boulder", not a chip, on the shoulders of our children- with home lives in disarray, uncaring educators, and opinionated adults. He gives a voice to the concerns and battles youngsters face. And thus, the beginning of *The Dirt Court.*

www.ingramcontent.com/pod-product-compliance
Lightning Source LLC
Chambersburg PA
CBHW020020030726
47499CB00007B/2193